W9-AUK-261

UNPLANNED CONNECTIONS

A Novel by

Peter Schmotzer

Sometimes it takes more strength to let go
Than it does to hold on

Chapter 1

Click

Ron McQuillen knew as soon as he pulled the trigger, it would be over. That is, everything *bad* would be over. His mistakes. His losses. His miserable life.

He had held the gun for so long it felt like it'd become an extension of himself. Postponing the inevitable was getting tiresome.

He remembered the final glimpse of his wife as she left the house. The last time he saw her she was stepping outside, holding their one-year old son, Bradley, her brown hair being whipped by the wind.

"Love you," she hollered.

"You, too."

He wished he had said more. He felt like their life as a family had only begun. He wished he had looked into her eyes and told her he loved her, so that she knew he meant it, because . . . just because.

That was months ago, but it felt like a lifetime. For Ron, they'd been apart for far too long. But as soon as he pulled the trigger, they'd be together again.

The morning sun lit the room, and the maple tree outside the window glowed in its fall attire. The edge of Ron's mouth twitched when he focused on the toy airplane sitting on the window sill. Some mornings, it almost glowed when the rays filtered through the leaves and struck it just right. The small plane looked out of place, but he had set it there a week ago to remind him that flying was always a chance to see life and the world from a new perspective. Unfortunately, he no longer believed there was anything to see and his perspective had only altered from gray to black.

The police said they'd call once the accident report was complete, but that didn't matter. Ron already knew the outcome, and it was buried in two caskets.

As he lifted the gun, he squeezed his eyes shut. With determination, he pressed the muzzle against his head so hard that, in minutes, a bruise would form if he changed his mind.

He pulled the trigger and heard the click, then silence. He pressed the muzzle against his head even harder and pulled the trigger. It didn't click this time; it felt cold and dead. The gun had never misfired before.

He screamed and pointed the gun toward the floor and pulled the trigger again.

This time it fired, the reverberation shuddering through his body. There was a small hole in the splintered wood floor where the bullet entered, and his ears rang from the loud discharge. Smoke from the chamber stung his eyes, and his nose filled with the acrid odor of burnt powder. He had only loaded one bullet since there wouldn't be any need for a

second round. He saw the reflection of a broken man in the dresser mirror, and he threw the gun at it. It crashed into the mirror, and he watched his reflection crumble as the shattered glass fell.

He leaned his head against his forearm and wept. *I'm cursed.*

Ron sprung up and walked down the dim hallway and through the messy kitchen. He yanked the door to the garage open and slammed his fist against the button to open the outer garage door. As the motor hummed and the door opened, he walked to the blue pickup truck and got in. He hadn't bothered to pull the service door shut behind him. He wasn't coming back.

He cranked the engine and it came to life. He slammed the truck into reverse and floored the accelerator. The tires spun on the concrete as the truck lurched out of the garage and he stomped on the brake. Ron slammed the gear selector into drive and floored it. The engine revved, but the truck didn't budge. Ron swore, then noticed the gear selector had slipped into neutral. Again, he slammed it into drive and floored it. This time the truck lunged forward. Stones spat from the gravel driveway as Ron tore toward the main road. A few seconds later, he felt the ABS pulsate when he slammed on the brakes.

He barely glanced both ways, then stomped on the

gas. The tires spat gravel until they squealed upon reaching the pavement of the road. A tractor-trailer truck blared its horn as it passed the other way. Ron cursed the semi. It reminded him of the one that had crushed the minivan his wife and son were in. *At least they didn't suffer.* That's what the doctor at the hospital said. It didn't make Ron feel any better. Through swollen eyes, he focused as well as he could. The afternoon sun sparsely penetrated the canopy of large trees that shielded the road. In places where fall leaves had surrendered to their fate, random patches of yellow glistened on the pavement.

Ron wondered why the gun hadn't fired.

A few miles later, he parked the truck outside his rental hanger at the local airport. As he got out of the truck, he heard the noise of a small aircraft departing. Normally, he would crane his neck to see if it was a local plane he would recognize. Not today.

He walked toward the hanger where his small Cessna resided. He knew that if he dove the plane into a nearby lake, it would all be over. There was no chance of *this* plan misfiring.

At the hanger door, he sorted through his keys until he found the one that unlocked the padlock. After the padlock yielded, he tossed it to the ground. He pushed on the hanger door to roll it back. It protested as moaning metal scraped against wheels that cried for oil. Then he rolled the other side open.

The white with red striped Cessna was where he had

parked it. The last flight had been with his wife while her sister babysat for them. She had wanted to go up to take photos of the summer landscape. She had planned to send copies of the best ones back home to her folks in Chicago. Here in Ohio's Amish country, life was far more tranquil for the McQuillens, and a few fabulous shots from God's perspective would help differentiate from the hustle and bustle of the city.

Ron kicked the chocks away from the front tires and unlocked the left door. After opening it, he reached inside and released the parking brake. He removed the tow bar through the small cargo door and latched it to the axle of the front wheel. He stood in front of the plane and pulled on the bar. Gradually, the plane rolled forward, its momentum increasing slowly as it rolled out of the hanger.

"Need a hand there?"

Ron looked over his shoulder and saw the source of the interruption about thirty feet away. He didn't recognize the stranger who looked to be similar in age to himself. Thin sideburns mixed with otherwise thick, black hair. A beige, long-sleeved shirt was tucked into what looked to be new jeans. A weathered brown leather coat was slung over his shoulder. Ron noticed the man's boots and instinctively focused behind him to see if there might be a horse nearby.

"Thanks, but no. I'm just going up for a solo flight."

The man's head tilted up. "Beautiful day for it."

Yeah, beautiful day to die, Ron thought. He surreptitiously watched the man from the corner of his eye as he loosened the tow bar. The man didn't budge.

Ron stood in front of the plane with the tow bar in hand. "You need something?"

The man gently nodded. "A lift."

Ron's brow furled. "If you wait around long enough, you'll find someone who can help you out. Sorry."

The man spoke as he slowly approached. "I was hoping you would. I need to get down to the Zanesville airport. It's only-"

Ron cut him off. "I know where Zanesville is!" With a tight grip, he raised the tow bar a few inches. "Do I look like taxi driver?" He gestured toward the next building. "Sam practically lives in that hanger. He's probably cleaning his plane again. Door's on the other side, so walk around and see for yourself." Ron figured as soon as the stranger dropped the conversation and left, he could hop in the Cessna and get out of there.

"It's kind of urgent," the man said as he took a few steps toward Ron, who felt like he was gripping the tow bar tight enough to crush the metal. Then he noticed the man's eyes. They weren't threatening. They seemed more empathetic than anything else, but that was no match for Ron's anger.

Ron thought of swinging the tow bar at the man to show he wasn't welcome, but he felt the tension gradually drain. Maybe he could do one good deed before checking out. A flight to Zanesville would only take about twenty minutes.

But he didn't want to come across as careless. Who would allow a complete stranger into his airplane without knowing something, anything, about the passenger? As if the man was reading Ron's mind, he spoke.

"Name's Mike," he said as he closed the distance between them with an outstretched arm.

Ron reflexively shook Mike's hand. "Ronald. Ronald McQuillen." The stranger's demeanor was disarming. "Call me Ron."

"Good to know you, Ron."

"I didn't notice you until I was pulling my plane out. How'd you get here?"

"Would you believe I flew in?"

"You just hitchhike from airport to airport?"

"Something like that."

"Tell me, Mike, why should I trust you? How do I know you aren't a serial killer who's going to whack me and push me out of my own plane from ten thousand feet?" The irony of his question made Ron feel somewhat foolish, given his plan. Part of him welcomed this distraction from his original intention and part of him rued the moment he first saw Mike. He knew he was merely delaying what he needed to do. Anne and Bradley were waiting.

Mike laughed. "Honestly, I can't say you don't. But I believe a man is only as good as his word, and I'll give you my word that I have no such intention."

Ron thought for a moment. "I don't suppose you know how to fly."

"Airplanes? I've held the yoke for straight and level but that's about it."

Ron sighed. He had been thinking maybe he could just step out of the plane when they were at altitude and then Mike could take things from there. He had loved airplanes since he was a young boy and had models of airplanes and flying magazines in his room. It would be a shame to waste such a nice plane, which felt like an odd thought since ten minutes earlier he was planning to crash it.

As he tried to rationalize denying the ride to the stranger, a white and gray dove's feather swirling in an eddy near the hanger caught his attention. It reminded him of when Anne had nursed an injured dove back to health. For an instant, the clouds within parted. He knew it was crazy, but he took the feather as a sign from Anne to give the stranger a lift. "All right. Let's go to Zanesville."

"Thank you."

Ron did a quick preflight. The oil level was normal, and there was more than enough fuel for the hop to Zanesville. He motioned to Mike to get in.

Fifteen minutes later they were a few thousand feet above the ground heading south. The sky was clear with a rich shade of blue. The earth below was painted with a canopy of reds, yellows, and browns. Even in Ron's distraught mental state, he appreciated the beauty of it. But it reminded him of his last flight with Anne. When he closed his eyes, he could hear her asking him to turn or tilt the plane to give her the best angle for the next photo. He could see her soaking in the landscape. He could even smell her hair.

Mike had been quiet, but Ron had been bombarded with so many of his own thoughts, he hadn't noticed. The hum of the engine was the only noise in the plane.

Normally, Ron would be far more talkative. He was good at keeping a conversation going with friends or strangers because he had so many interests. He found it easy to find commonalities which soon evolved into long-term friendships. He had become good friends with a waiter, Walt, at the local Bob Evans where he often had lunch. Walt was in school to become a counselor, but found himself torn between required study hours and quality time with his wife and twins. Ron helped him to find balance, and Anne had also encouraged him when she met with Ron for lunch. But after he lost his family, he no longer saw value in friendship. He ignored Walt's voicemails and often deleted them without listening. If loved ones could be lost too easily, then so could friends.

As a family counselor, he had helped people who were dealing with similar losses. But there was no way for Ron to counsel himself. He had met with one of his colleagues who tried to help. The meeting barely lasted for ten minutes before Ron broke into a tirade and stormed out. Afterwards, he felt foolish for calling the counselor a quack, given they pursued similar careers. Still, he had yet to apologize or return the counselor's phone calls or emails. Nor would he have the opportunity to do so after today's plan was complete. Too often, life's loose ends didn't wrap up as neat and tidy as a fiction novel he cynically thought.

Life had been good before he met Anne. Then it became great. Ron never considered himself particularly spiritual, but the night before he got married, he got down on his knees and thanked God for Anne. After they got married, life was grand. He swore to be the best husband he could for her. Once Bradley came along, their life together changed, but they both embraced the changes that came with being parents, and even hoped that Bradley would have a sibling in the near future. That was all stolen the instant the truck crashed into the side of the minivan. The cops had told Ron the occupants never stood a chance.

"I think you may be the quietest pilot I ever met," Mike said.

Ron didn't care what Mike thought. In another ten minutes, they'd be on the ground in Zanesville, and they'd never see each other again.

"I know it isn't my place," Mike said over the drone of the engine. "But sometimes it helps to talk to a stranger."

"What makes you think I need to talk?"

"Your eyes. They keep searching for answers. I appreciate you giving me a lift, so I'd be happy to listen."

"You don't owe me anything. Forget about it."

"Can you?"

"Can I what?"

"Forget about it."

"I will soon enough."

"How?"

Ron focused on the point where the cowling met the horizon. A trace of a smile touched the edges of his mouth for an instant as he remembered the first time he tried to teach his wife the basics of flying. *See the point where the horizon touches the cowling? Just keep the nose of the plane pitched so it stays right there and you'll maintain your altitude.*

Once they'd landed, they laughed over her brief lesson. She had constantly pushed or pulled the yoke causing the plane to pitch up and down like a roller coaster. He had given her more pointers during future flights, but she preferred to let him do the flying. Now, he didn't fly anymore because he didn't want to fly alone.

"Don't worry about it," Ron finally replied. He could feel Mike's eyes searching him for more, and the weight of his stare was making Ron uncomfortable. "Do I know you from somewhere?"

The delay in Mike's reply made Ron anxious. "We've never met if that's what you're asking."

"That's what I thought, and after I drop you off, we won't be meeting again."

"I'm sorry if I upset you," Mike said, and he resumed looking out the side window.

Ron had no interest in receiving counseling, whether it was on the ground, or in the one place where he always felt free – where he *used* to always feel free – in an airplane high above the problems he left behind. "We'll be landing soon." He was anxious to get rid of the stranger.

Ron reduced the throttle, which lowered the droning noise from the engine. He looked over and saw Mike looking out the side window toward the ground. Ron mused he was probably watching the interstate below. People driving through life on cruise, content going back and forth in the little ruts life had created for them. It reminded him of Sisyphus who pushed the rock up the hill only to have it roll back down. Life was meaningless to him now and there was no reason to sustain it. Once Mike was dropped off, Ron could finally do what he planned.

Ron lowered the first notch of flaps, and the plane slowly descended. He opened the throttle a bit to compensate for the extra drag created by the extended flaps.

"You're going straight in?" Mike asked.

"I don't see anyone around. There's no use wasting time flying the pattern. We'll land on runway 22."

"What about announcing your position?"

Ron looked at Mike. "You want to fly the plane? Are you suddenly a hot shot pilot?"

Mike looked back at Ron with a disarming countenance of calm and gently shook his head.

"Look buddy, I'm going to land, and we'll go our -" Ron saw Mike's mouth open and his eyes widened. Ron looked in the same direction as Mike and saw a twin-engine airplane flying toward them. It was only seconds away. The other plane was descending and the pilot probably didn't see the Cessna since Ron wasn't calling out his positions on the local frequency. Ron instinctively pushed the yoke forward while banking to the right, which pointed them at the ground. The stall horn went off for an instant and loose gear from the area behind the seats flew up and hit the ceiling. Ron swore as he fought to bring the plane out of the dive. He jammed the throttle to the firewall, pulled the yoke back and held his breath as the aircraft barely missed the treetops and started climbing again.

Mike watched Ron turn the radio on for the first time

and adjust it to the local frequency. Ron called out their position in the air traffic pattern and a few minutes later, the wheels chirped as the plane bounced down the runway. When he looked toward the aircraft parking ramp, Ron saw the low-wing aircraft they had narrowly missed. It looked like a Piper Seminole, a small twin engine airplane. A man, a woman, and two small kids were climbing out of it. A family.

Ron was surprised Mike hadn't said anything. He looked over and saw that Mike, too, was watching the people exit the other plane.

"Any landing you can walk away from is a good one," Mike said.

Ron didn't reply.

"It's not like anyone was looking to die today, so let's not worry about it."

Ron winced at the impact from Mike's words. He taxied the plane to the ramp, parked as far from the Piper aircraft as possible and cut the throttle.

"I have somewhere I need to be," Mike said as he opened the door. He stuck a foot out but turned to face Ron. "Thanks for the lift."

For the first time that day, Ron laughed. He shook his head and laughed harder. "I nearly kill you and these folks and you thank me? Are you insane?"

Mike smiled as he chuckled a bit. "No, but I'm alive, right?"

"Yeah, and so am . . ." Ron stopped talking. He searched his thoughts for clues with regards to what he knew about Mike. He suddenly wished he had engaged the man in more conversation.

Mike got out and walked quickly to leave the aircraft parking area.

Ron wished he could take off and continue with his original plan, but he knew he owed the other pilot an apology. He heard the man by the Piper Seminole yell something toward Mike, but over the wind, the words were muffled.

Chapter 2
The Next Leg

Ron gripped the door latch but hesitated. He saw the man from the other plane walking toward him. The man's fists were clenched and his footsteps landed solid and firm like those of a soldier. Ron unlatched the door and got out.

"What kind of flying was that?" the man yelled with arms spread, palms up.

Ron raised his hands halfway for an instant and looked away from the man.

The man got in Ron's face. "What were you doing up there? Do you even have a pilot's license?" His voice got louder, and he pointed behind him toward the Piper aircraft. "You nearly killed my family!"

Ron stepped back. He knew he had made a mistake that could've ended in tragedy.

"Jerry," the woman next to Piper yelled. "Let it go. The kids and I are fine. We need to go."

For the first time, Ron noticed the man's son. He reminded Ron of how he thought Bradley might have looked someday—if he had lived to grow older. For the past month, nearly every boy he saw reminded him of the son he no longer had. The thought of what nearly happened made him wince. The emotion was already knocked out of him when Jerry took a swing and hit him. He fell to the ground.

The world teetered between fuzzy and black. Ron heard Jerry's wife yelling as she ran toward them. Jerry was hovering over Ron screaming like he was about to commit murder. Ron lay in pain, but relaxed. He could taste blood. He didn't care. He could hear the couple fighting.

"Sarah, I'm not apologizing. You saw what this man did."

"Honey, please. You're scaring the kids. Just apologize and then we can go."

"Why should *I* apologize?"

"Your temper, honey, please," Sarah whispered. "Look at what you did to him. It's over."

Ron saw Jerry's eyes peer at him as if they saw through him and saw his worst.

"Come on, your brother's waiting," Sarah said.

Jerry looked at his wife. "I know."

Ron started regaining his senses and was able to discern his surroundings better. He looked at the two people above him.

"I'm leaving," Sarah said. She turned around and walked toward the Piper where the kids were still standing.

Ron saw the way Jerry looked at his wife and kids. The anger drained from Jerry's face, and his hands unclenched.

"I'm sorry," Ron said. He saw agitation return to Jerry's face when he looked back down at Ron.

"What'd you say?"

"I said I'm sorry. It was my mistake."

Ron could see the man was thinking. He hoped he wasn't going to kick him while he was down. Then again, he knew he probably deserved it. He envied the fact that Jerry had a family, and he was angry with himself for nearly knocking them out of the sky. He wondered if the man knew how blessed he was.

Again, Jerry looked over toward his family. "I'll be right there." Sarah and the kids had gathered their bags and were walking toward the parking lot. Jerry held onto his right hand and rubbed it with the other. Ron could see that his hand was red and presumed it ached from the hit.

Ron gingerly rubbed his jaw. "Pretty nice hook you've got."

"Pretty hard jaw you've got. I shouldn't have done that. Sorry, man."

"I earned it."

Jerry nodded with a slight smile. "Well, it's been a hard day and it's going to get harder so I need to get going." He extended his uninjured hand. Ron took it, and Jerry helped him up.

"Thanks."

"Sure. I need to go." Jerry turned to leave but only got a few steps away before Ron spoke.

"Hold on a second. Why did you say the day was going to get harder?"

Jerry stopped but didn't turn around to face Ron. He took a deep breath. "We're only here because my brother's in the hospital."

"I'm sorry."

Jerry slowly shook his head. "It wouldn't be so hard if he hadn't tried to commit suicide."

Ron looked at the ground.

"I'll never understand why people do that." Jerry turned around and squinted as he spoke. "When you have people who count on you, who love you?" His arms were outstretched. "Why would a man ever do that?"

Ron's continued to look at the ground. "Something must've happened. What did he lose?"

"That's just the thing. He lost his retirement fund due to some bad investments in the stock market. But he's young. He can still work to earn it back."

"He has a family?"

"They just had a baby boy."

The words knocked the wind out of Ron and he crumpled to the tarmac.

"Whoa! Hey man, you okay?" Jerry ran over and knelt over Ron.

Ron lifted his head. "I lost my son."

"Are you looking for him? Is that where the other guy ran off to?"

"No. He was killed with my wife in a car accident. A semi-truck ran into the side of their minivan and . . ." Ron groaned.

Jerry's shoulders slumped. "I'm so sorry." He put his hand on Ron's shoulder for a moment and then grabbed his hand. "Here, let me help you up." He pulled and Ron stumbled to his feet.

"This is getting to be a habit," Ron mumbled.

Jerry didn't say anything. Ron could see he was looking him over and then back to where his family had exited the ramp. Ron wanted to get back into his plane and take off. Learning that Jerry's brother could even think of ending his own life while his family was alive was unimaginable to him. It was like a gut punch. It only added to his sense of worthlessness. The world was broken and there was no way he could help to fix it. Any of it. It would be a better place without him.

He had thought giving Mike a lift would reward him with a purifying feeling that would make his reunion with Anne and Bradley the natural conclusion of his life. But his carelessness had nearly cost more lives, and he felt the sudden urge to apologize to Sarah. A simple apology would cleanse him of his earlier misdeed and clear him for his final action.

"I don't even know your name. Mine's Jerry Haines."

"Ron. Ron McQuillen."

They shook hands. "Glad to know you, Ron."

"I need to apologize to your wife, Jerry. I'll do that and be on my way."

Jerry hesitated. "You don't have to do that. She'll be fine."

"What about the kids? They should understand that when a man makes a mistake, he does the right thing by owning up to it and apologizing."

Ron could see Jerry was surprised by his words. "I think that'd be all right."

"Thank you."

"Follow me." Ron followed Jerry into the parking lot. He looked for Mike, but the man was nowhere to be seen. As they approached a silver Toyota sedan, Ron saw Sarah getting the kids fastened into car seats.

"Honey," Jerry called out.

Sarah poked her head out of the car. Ron could see the look of apprehension on her face when she saw him with her husband. He walked beside Jerry to try to make it obvious he wasn't a threat.

"Wait here," Jerry said. "I'll talk to her for a second, then you can come over."

"Okay." Ron stopped and stood with his hands in his pockets. He felt like the world was watching him, judging him, like everyone knew what his intentions were and that he should be ashamed. It angered him and made him feel more defiant. He was anxious to get the apology over with.

Jerry spoke with Sarah for a few seconds. He waved at Ron, who walked over and joined them. "I'll let the two of you talk," Jerry said. He poked his head in the backseat of the car to talk with the kids.

Ron walked over to the driver's side of the car and Sarah reluctantly followed. She looked at Ron inquisitively. He could see the discomfort on her face. She crossed her arms.

"I just wanted to apologize. I wasn't paying attention up there and it nearly ended in disaster."

She looked around as if the right words for a reply were hiding. "Thank you."

Ron could hear Jerry's upbeat voice and the children's muted laughter. "That's all I wanted to say."

She looked at him with searching eyes.

"I need to go." He turned and walked back toward the tarmac. He heard footsteps approaching from behind and Jerry stopped in front of him at the edge of the parking lot.

"I appreciate what you did back there."

"Just trying to make things right."

"That you did."

Ron saw the orange windsock over by the runway getting pushed by the breeze. He couldn't wait to get out of there. "I think I should-"

"Come with us," Jerry interrupted.

"What?"

"Come with us."

"No, I, uh . . . honestly, I don't think that's a good idea. I need to be going."

"Going? Going where? You just got here. This won't take long at all."

"I have a, uh . . ."

Jerry smiled. "Yeah, you have no excuse you can think of, right?"

Ron deflated.

Jerry slapped him on the back. "You'll be doing me a personal favor." He waited a few moments, but Ron didn't yield. "And I promise not to hit you again," he joked.

Ron looked at him through squinted eyes.

Jerry lowered his voice. "And if you do, it will help me to prove to my wife that I'm getting better."

"Getting better?"

"Yeah, she says I have some anger issues." Jerry looked away. "It's kind of getting in the way of my job. Or it could if word gets out."

"What's that have to do with your job?"

"I'm a pastor at our church."

Chapter 3

A New Friend

Ron saw Sarah's eyes nearly pop out of her head as he and Jerry approached the car again.

"Jerry, what's going on?"

"Sarah, honey. We didn't have a formal introduction. This is Ron."

Ron extended his hand. "Ron McQuillen."

Sarah reluctantly took his hand. "Sarah," she said while she looked at her husband.

Jerry nodded toward the car. "And that's Ethan and Avery in the backseat." He looked at his wife. "Ron's going to join us."

Ron could see Sarah was uncomfortable with the situation. He noticed how her eyelids fluttered when she spoke to Jerry again.

"Um, okay." She looked at Ron. "Mr. McQuillen, you don't owe us anything." She looked at her husband. "Now really, Jerry, what's going on?"

Jerry put his hands on his wife's shoulders and looked into her eyes. "I know this sounds crazy. But Ron's been through a very traumatic event. I think he's come into our lives for a reason." Ron saw him whisper something into her ear. She nodded, smiled at Ron nervously, then got in the back of the car and maneuvered her petite frame between the car seats.

"You have shotgun," Jerry said to Ron as he climbed into the driver's seat.

Ron walked around the back of the car. He could see Sarah talking to the children. Even though he couldn't hear her, he could see she leaned close to the kids and must have been talking in a low voice, as if Ron was already seated in front of her. He opened the door and plopped into the passenger seat.

Fifteen minutes later, Ron and Jerry's family were on the interstate. After crossing over the river, Jerry took the first exit and headed north. Minutes later, they were pulling into the hospital parking lot. Jerry twisted in his seat to face the children. "Ready to see Uncle Robert? What do you say, Ethan?"

"Will he have animal crackers for us?"

"No, grandpa and grandma are the ones who always bring animal crackers."

"What about you, Avery?" Jerry reached back and tickled her foot for a second, and she giggled.

She had been humming a song that Ron had practically memorized during the brief trip. It was a short song and had been played four times. He welcomed the distraction from his prior thoughts, even if it was just a silly tune for toddlers. Jerry and Sarah got the kids out of the car seats. Moments later, they walked through the automatic doors, and Jerry stopped to talk to the receptionist.

When they entered, Ron noticed that Sarah had directed Ethan toward the elevators. She was holding Avery. The trio stood next to one of the faux ficus trees that were on either side of the elevator doors. Sarah had a look of concern on her face. Ron wondered what Jerry had whispered to her back at the airport. She seemed like a good mom, a protective mom. His years as a counselor had shown him that trust took a long time to earn but could be lost in an instant. He wondered why these people had shown so much trust in him so soon.

Jerry turned around. "Room 308. Let's go." Ron followed Jerry to the elevators.

Sarah saw them approaching and pressed the Up arrow. No one said anything on the elevator. Ethan looked up at Ron with curiosity. A few seconds later, they exited on the third floor. Jerry stopped to talk to the nurse at the receptionist desk for a few seconds. Ron saw the nurse point.

Jerry stopped outside the entrance to Room 308. "Give me a minute to see how he's doing."

"I hope he's awake," Sarah said. She was still holding Avery. Ethan latched onto her leg when they stopped. Ron could see fear in the boy's eyes. The distress reminded him of the last time he was at the hospital. There was good reason to be afraid.

The only sounds that came from the room after Jerry went in were whispers. Ron was near Sarah and the kids; his back was against the wall. He feigned a smile at a passing nurse whose shoes allowed her to slip by in silence. She smiled warmly back at him, then more energetically toward the kids.

A minute later, Jerry exited. "He wants to see you."

Ron watched for Sarah to go in.

Jerry looked at Ron. "Ron, Robert wants to see you."

"What? Me?" He shook his head. "Why me? I don't even . . ."

Jerry stepped closer to Ron and put a hand on his shoulder.

"It's okay." He stepped back and motioned with his hand toward the open doorway. "Go ahead."

Sarah looked at Ron and shrugged.

Ethan looked up at him. "I'm hungry for animal crackers."

"You'll get animal crackers later," Sarah said.

Ron's legs felt heavy as he slowly entered the room. His thoughts flashed back to the moment when he had gotten the call to come to the hospital back home a month ago. On the way there, he pictured what he'd say to his wife. He could envision her lying in a hospital bed with wires and tubes sustaining her with their son in a bed nearby. That would be awful, but he had prepared himself for it. It was after he had arrived at the hospital that he found out his family was dead.

The feeling here was different. The afternoon sun shone through the large windows and lit every corner.

Flowers with bright colors were on a table at the foot of the bed. Cards were on the windowsill.

An IV tube disappeared into Robert's arm. There weren't too many wires that Ron noticed. He had expected a much graver scenario. It made him wonder what Robert had done. With no obvious physical injuries, Ron suspected an overdose of pills.

Robert turned his head as Ron approached. The remnants of his thinning, dark hair were disheveled, and the lines in his face hinted at weariness. He reached out, and Ron reacted by slowing his pace.

"Thanks for coming," Robert said.

Ron nodded. His conflicting thoughts made him want to grab Robert and shake some sense into the man for attempting to leave his family this way. He could feel his pulse quickening as he took the last few steps toward the bedside.

"Why did you want to see me?"

"Jerry told me about your loss. I'm sorry."

Ron searched Robert's eyes and saw that they were sincere. At the same time, he noticed Robert was searching his own eyes for something. He wondered if Robert had had a change of heart regarding his own situation. Surely, the man must appreciate what he'd nearly lost. A part of Ron wanted to trade places with him. Robert would be able to return to his family. For Ron, that choice didn't exist. All that remained was the pain. Ron looked over the man lying before him and motioned with his hands. "Why'd you do it?"

Robert slowly turned his head away. "Honestly? The shame." He paused for a moment. "I couldn't face my wife so I took the only alternative I knew."

"You had a family. You *still* have a family."

"I know. Now I know."

"Now you know?" Ron echoed.

Robert turned his head to look at Ron again. "Now, yes. Jerry briefed me about your situation. When you entered, I saw it in your face. What I nearly put my wife through and what my son would be suffering through for the years to come. That's why I asked Jerry to send you in. I know it probably seems strange to you, but your story and that look on your face is what I needed. And don't ask me why, I'm still sorting it all out in my own messed up head."

"Then you know nothing."

"What?"

"You shouldn't need to walk over the edge to find out what happens when you hit the ground. Haven't a thousand other people already done it?"

Robert sighed. "I'm afraid I was a slow learner this time."

Ron looked down at the floor. It was remarkably clean, even in the bright sunlight. "So you're okay now?"

"Yeah, I am. I mean I'm going to be, eventually. Thanks."

Ron smiled for an instant and nodded.

"But I need to ask you something."

"What?"

"How'd you get that bruise on your temple?"

Ron instinctively felt the side of his head where he had pressed the gun earlier. "I don't remember."

Robert scratched the side of his head. "I've been a cop for nearly twenty years. I've seen that type of bruising before."

Ron's breathing increased. He looked away from Robert.

"So, Ron, tell me. Are *you* going to be okay?"

"Don't worry about me."

"I choose to."

"There's no point to it."

"From what you've told me, there's plenty to it. We all have people in our lives who care about us, and who we need to care about, right?"

"So is that all we need to do here? You and I have a nice chat, sing Kumbaya, and everyone goes home happy?" Ron stepped over to Robert's bed, gripped the bedrails, and leaned close to his face. He spoke through gritted teeth. "For you, it may work that way. You get to go home. For me, my home was my family. Capisce?"

"No."

"No?" Ron stood but kept both hands on the bedrail.

"We go on no matter what. That was my mistake, trying to quit. Now I have a second chance. I don't know why I do, but I have no intention of wasting it."

"Lucky you."

"And you. I think you've got one, too. I hope you don't waste it."

Ron was tired of the conversation and was ready to say anything to get out of the room. "It's time for me to go."

"I hope we talk again. Soon."

"Sure." Ron left the room. To him, the conversation was senseless. He was angry with Robert, the fool, and a lucky fool at that.

Ron expected to find Jerry and his family waiting outside the doorway, but they were gone. He walked to the reception desk and spoke with the nurse who said she saw them take the elevator, and that they may have gone to the cafeteria on the first floor. Ron thanked her, walked over to the elevator and hit the Down arrow. When his hand fell by his side, he felt a lump in his pocket. He remembered that his phone was there, and that it was probably still off. He had turned it off last night because he didn't want to talk to anyone. Nonetheless, he was in the habit of always carrying it.

He found his mood slightly more somber now, so he pulled the phone out and turned it on. After a few seconds, a message box popped up stating there was a voicemail.

"Excuse me, sir. No cell phone calls are allowed in the hospital," the nurse said from behind him.

"Right, sorry." The elevator doors opened and he pocketed the phone as he entered.

Chapter 4
The Preacher

Ron heard the familiar elevator tone, and the doors opened. He stepped out and saw the wall placard with directions to various areas of the hospital. He went in the direction of the arrow pointing to the cafeteria.

The cafeteria was brightly lit due to the large windowpanes that ran from the floor to the ceiling, and unlike the rest of the hospital, the floor was covered with beige ceramic tile. Thick metal arms thrust out from beneath tables to support the attached chairs. The area was sparsely populated with visitors. A pair of doctors in blue scrubs sat on either side of a table next to one of the windows.

Ron spotted Sarah and walked toward the table where she was seated. As he neared, she pointed to an empty seat with a wrapped sandwich and bottled water.

"Glad you could join me," she said. A crumpled wrapper was on the red tray in front of her. She fidgeted with a half-finished cup of coffee.

"Where's everyone else?"

"Jerry took the kids to the park outside. At first he wanted me to, but I said I wanted to get some lunch first. I was hoping you would join me."

"Thanks." Ron's neglected hunger pangs suddenly surfaced. He sat and unwrapped the turkey sandwich. He was perplexed by Sarah's changed demeanor and wondered what had changed within her.

He took a bite of the sandwich. "This is great, thank you," he said while chewing.

"Sure." Sarah leaned in toward him. "I've been thinking. Tell me, Ron. Why did Robert want to talk to *you*? Why would he want to talk to a stranger?"

Ron remembered what Mike had said to him earlier, that sometimes it's easier to talk to a stranger. "I don't know. I must admit, it does seem odd."

"What did the two of you discuss? It was their father, wasn't it," she said matter-of-factly as she leaned back in the seat. "I knew it. You know, that man puts so much pressure on those boys, it's a wonder they can even think straight."

"I don't think Robert was thinking straight."

Sarah threw her hands up. "My point exactly."

"But he never mentioned anything about his dad. Only that he was sorry he let his family down."

Sarah nodded. "He's had a hard life. His wife has been looking for work since getting laid off last year while she was pregnant with their son. Did he tell you they recently had a son?"

"Jerry told me at the airport."

"Then it has to make you wonder what was going through his head doesn't it? I mean to make a man try to take his own life."

Ron stopped chewing for an instant. He shook his head. He started chewing again but now he had a lump in his throat.

"So, if it wasn't about their father, why did he want to see you?"

Ron reflected on their discussion and on Robert's observation of his bruise. "I think he knew we had something in common. I lost my family, and he nearly lost his."

"Did you talk some sense into him?"

"I don't think I did anything for him." Ron shrugged. "Maybe I did. I don't know." Ron took another moment to think about their discussion. "What I do know is that he's going to be okay."

For the first time, Sarah saw the hint of a smile on Ron's face.

"I think we may have helped each other. Odd as that sounds, I'd say that's what happened."

Sarah searched Ron's face for more information while he uncapped the bottle of water and took a large swig. She took a sip of coffee. "You know how Jerry convinced me to let you come with us to the hospital? He said you were good for his anger issues. Usually he just yells a lot. Today was the first time I saw him hit someone."

"Has he ever threatened you or the kids?"

"No, but when he yells, Ethan gets scared, runs off to his room and slams the door. It's not good for our son to be exposed to such anger. But what makes it harder for Jerry is his job."

"Preacher, right?"

"A pastor."

"There's a difference?"

The corner of Sarah's lip twitched as her eyes scanned the ceiling for a second. "I think people think of a preacher as someone who screams fire and brimstone from the pulpit, but Jerry really has a gift. He really knows how to reach people. It's why I married him."

Ron wondered why Jerry hadn't been able to help his own brother, but he didn't want to broach the topic if it could be avoided.

"I'm afraid the church elders would replace him if they found out about his temper."

"What's he doing about it?"

"Well, flying for one. That seems to sooth him more than anything else. He just loves it. So does Ethan. I was nervous about it at first, but he had taken me up right after we started dating."

Ron noticed her convincing and warm smile. She had a smile that could sell toothpaste to people without teeth.

"And when he proposed, it was on a clear evening, right at sunset at five thousand feet. I thought that was so romantic. None of my girlfriends' husbands did anything like that."

Ron smiled. His eyebrows rose. "Congratulations, that's a wonderful memory."

"But the flying is also part of the problem."

"Oh?"

"The airplane is his dad's, a retired airline pilot. He started teaching Jerry how to fly when he was just a teenager. And he wanted Jerry to become a pilot just like him. When Jerry told him he wanted to be a pastor, his dad nearly disowned him. He's better now, but it's still a sore spot." Sarah slowly rotated the coffee cup between her thumb and forefinger. "You know what's really a shame? I never would have met him if he had pursued a career as a pilot. I was a PK, and I wanted to marry a man who was a pastor."

"A PK?"

"Preacher's kid."

"But you didn't want to marry a preacher, just a pastor."

"Well, oh, you know what I mean."

Ron laughed as he nodded. Sarah laughed, too.

"How are you and his folks?"

"I'm the mother of their grandkids so that counts for something. But sometimes I can feel the resentment as if I stole their son from them."

"I'm sorry."

Sarah shrugged. "They're good to Ethan and Avery. They make the kids happy and that makes me happy. So I don't make any issue of it. Things are never perfect, but we take it day by day. And we have each other, which is everything."

Ron thought of how well his wife got along with everyone. A twinge of pain pierced his heart as he remembered how much he missed her.

Sarah noticed the change in Ron's demeanor. "Oh, gosh, Ron, I'm so sorry. I should . . ."

Ron held his hand up. "Forget it." He shook his head. He looked into Sarah's eyes and saw her searching the room for words.

Sarah sighed. "Hey, she'll always live in your memory, right?"

Ron saw the sincerity in her moist eyes even though he found her words had the antithesis of the intended effect. He pounded his fist on the table. Every head in the room turned to face their table. "Live? The one thing she'll *never* do again is live. Any memory I have of her today will fade even dimmer tomorrow until it's just a shadow of what used to be my wife. I'll have nothing real, just these contrived memories where my subconscious controls her like a puppet - makes her smile or cry."

Sarah was shaking her head. "Ron, I'm so-"

He cut her off angrily. "Forget it." He got up. "I need a ride back to the airport." He could see Sarah was upset, but he really didn't care.

Sarah rose, too. "Okay, I'm sure Jerry will give you a lift." She walked over and put a hand on his shoulder. "Ron, I'm terribly sorry. I won't tell you I know how you feel because it's not true. And if my words are only hurting you, then I won't say anything else."

Ron nodded. "Let's find Jerry." He left the cafeteria with Sarah following.

She looked away from him to grab a tissue from her purse. She dabbed at the tears on her face.

Ron asked a passing nurse where the park was. A minute later, he exited the hospital.

"There you are," Jerry called out as he gave Ethan another push on the swing.

Ron was quiet as he approached Jerry.

"Everything okay?"

"Would you give me a lift back to the airport," Ron said curtly.

"Of course." Jerry surveyed Ron. "What's wrong?"

Ron looked away and his eyes fell upon a young couple casually walking hand-in-hand. They looked happy. He'd never be happy again. He was so tired of thinking this way, but it seemed that everyone and everything reminded him of what he no longer had. Internally, there was a constant struggle between wanting to forget and wanting to remember. His lips pursed as he reflected on what was missing in his life. He thought he had been rather clear to Jerry earlier, but now he wasn't sure. He was sure that he didn't care to discuss it or how he planned to handle it. He knew that his plan would fix things for him in the immediacy, which was all that mattered. "I, uh, just need to get going, that's all."

"Okay," Jerry said slowly. "You hungry? My wife's in the cafeteria."

Ron thought Jerry was stalling. "Are you going to take me to the airport? If not, just say so and I'll get a cab."

"No, no, I'll give you a lift." He saw Sarah approaching them. "Hi, hon."

She raised a hand and waved.

When she joined them, Jerry asked her to watch the kids while he took Ron back to the airport. Ron avoided looking her in the eye. As he was walking to the car with Jerry, he felt like he should apologize to her. His intentions wouldn't allow him to apologize tomorrow or any other time for that matter. But then he thought of how her words hurt him, and he rationalized his actions. It was the type of justification he would never advise to a counseling client.

Jerry tried to break the silence during the drive. Ron chose to stare out the window. The world passed by, and he couldn't wait to stop watching it. The sooner he could fly a few thousand feet off the ground, the sooner he could dive at top speed into the first lake he spotted and end this. No more suffering, no more pain. There was no antidote to his condition, and he just wanted it all to stop.

Jerry turned the car into the airport parking lot and parked. He remained quiet. Ron sensed Jerry's tension and anger. They both sat there while the engine idled.

"I wish there was something I could do," Jerry said while he gripped the wheel. He looked over at Ron, who slowly shook his head. "For me, that was a tough drive."

Ron stared forward at the entrance to the building. Aircraft rentals and flying lessons were advertised on a banner next to the door.

"I wish you wouldn't ignore me, Ron. But I'm going to tell you something. I believe everything happens for a reason."

"Or maybe things happen because that's how it is. That's all there is. Nothing more."

"I don't have any answers about what happened to your family. I only know that I'm very sorry about what happened. I'm not going to explain away anything, but I will tell you I'm grateful you came into my life."

Ron's breathing increased, and his fists and chest tightened.

"I know this sounds selfish, but do you have any idea how hard it is being a pastor? People with all kinds of problems are always looking to you for answers and calling at all times of the day and night. With my job I also do counseling." Jerry threw his hands up. "It's like people believe being a pastor gives you the red phone directly to God and all of life's answers. Would you believe that on the flight here today, I was dreading the hospital visit with my brother? I had no idea what I was going to say to him. Here I am, the guy who's supposed to have all the answers, and I had nothing. I felt like a complete fraud."

Ron finally looked at him. "So?"

"So, I prayed about it, and you came along and did what I could not. You helped him. You were the answer to my prayers."

Ron rolled his eyes. "That's ridiculous. You don't know that."

"I do."

"How?"

"How was he when you left him?"

Ron was quiet. He saw Jerry searching his face.

Jerry smiled. "He was fine, wasn't he? You did that. You saved him. You helped him to see what was important in his life."

"You sound awfully sure of yourself."

Jerry chuckled. "And me. Would you believe you helped me, too?"

"I did?"

"You helped with something I've been praying about lately, my anger problems. This is important to my wife and I because it's been affecting our marriage. I've been worried about losing my temper in public and losing my job, too."

"So that's it? I'm here to help you like some pathetic seeing eye dog waiting to be put down when it's used up?"

Jerry's head recoiled an inch, then he squinted at Ron. "What do you mean? How can you think such a thing?"

Ron leaned toward Jerry. "When a man loses his family, everything around him haunts him like a ghost. Everything reminds him of what he no longer has. And every friend you ever had looks at you while having an anxiety attack over what to say."

"I don't understand, Ron. I just wanted you to know that today you really helped my family and I'm grateful. I want you to know that life goes on tomorrow in spite of what happens today."

"You have no idea." Ron laughed as he dragged his hand over his face.

"What's so funny?" Jerry asked.

"Did you hear me?"

"Ron, I'm listening."

"Then listen. This morning I awoke from a dream. I was with my wife and I was begging her to stay. She looked me in the eyes, cradled my head and said she would never leave me. I pleaded with her not to go, but she laughed at me and said not to worry, that she'd be dead soon and so would our son. She laughed as she left, and I tried to run after her. I cried out to her not to go. I screamed and told her what would happen. But she laughed as she backed the minivan out of the garage. I tried to run after them, but my feet were heavy and I couldn't move. When I woke up, I knew it was a nightmare because Anne was *never* cruel like that. It was like a demon had possessed the precious memory I had left of her." Ron looked at Jerry through a cataract of tears. "That wasn't her at all Jerry, I swear to you. She'd never do that in real life, but she did in this dream. I don't want to remember her like that. If that's how my thoughts are going to torture me, what's the point of going on? If God would just allow me to find her for a minute, the nightmare would be scared off."

Jerry leaned over with open arms to hug Ron, but Ron pushed him away. "I'm sorry, Ron. I'm so sorry."

"It's not fair." Ron sobbed.

"It's not."

After a minute, Ron wiped his eyes. "But that's all I have to look forward to."

The car was quiet for a few minutes until Jerry pulled out a small notepad from the map pocket, wrote on it, tore the top page off and gave it to Ron. "I want you to call. Anytime, okay?"

Ron's hurt was chased away by thoughts of the future. He pictured the daily pain he would have to endure until the end of time, or at least until the end of his life. He took the paper from Jerry and looked at it for a few seconds. He stuffed it into his front pocket. Then he looked at the man who had a wife and children waiting for him. His jaw clenched. "I need to go."

Jerry held his hand out, and Ron shook it. He only needed to maintain appearances for a few more minutes. He quickly exited the car and walked alongside the building toward the ramp where his Cessna was parked. There was no future for him, just a quick flight and a quick dive into a lake in the middle of nowhere. Nothing on earth would cure his pain faster. He wouldn't be missed any more than a pail of water stolen from the ocean. He took a deep breath as he finalized his decision. It wouldn't be long now, and there was no one around to stop him this time.

He walked onto the tarmac and saw his plane up ahead. He stopped.

Standing next to it was Mike.

Chapter 5

Toledo

"Hey!" Mike hollered across the tarmac. His leather jacket was slung over one shoulder.

The sound hit Ron like a gale that stopped him as he questioned his own eyes. "You got to be kidding me," he mumbled. It felt like déjà vu.

Mike waved at him to come over. "I had her filled up for you."

Ron walked over to the plane. "The tanks are full?"

"See for yourself."

Ron put his foot on the wing spare step and hoisted himself to view the top of the wing. He uncapped the tank and saw the fuel level. "Why?" he asked abruptly.

"Figured I owed you some petrol for the trip, right? And that roller-coaster ride at the end was worth a few extra bucks."

Ron rolled his eyes. This guy was nuts. He put the fuel cap back on and stepped down onto the tarmac. "So are we done?" He sighed.

Mike looked out toward the runway. "Sure is a nice day for a flight. A long flight over the state would be beautiful on a day like this. Perfect, really."

Ron grew more annoyed that Mike was delaying his plans. "Here's the deal, Mike. We're even, and you don't owe me anything. So, just leave it at that."

"I was going to ask you . . ."

"Mike, leave!" Ron yelled.

"What's the rush?"

"Where I'm going, you can't go and I don't want company!"

Mike looked at Ron inquisitively but held his tongue. The breeze increased enough to brush through his hair while the sun reflected the sheen off his forehead, as if he'd worked up a sweat.

Ron stood firmly in hopes that Mike would walk away. He noticed one pocket of Mike's leather jacket was bulging. Neither man spoke for another minute until curiosity finally got the best of Ron. "It looks like fuel isn't the only thing you got."

"Pardon?"

Ron's head bobbed. "Your coat pocket. What's in it?"

Mike laughed. "I'm glad you asked. It's a great story."

"Skip to the end," Ron interrupted. "What's in the pocket?"

Mike smiled as he unslung the jacket from his shoulder. He unbuttoned the pocket and produced a baseball. The word *AM* had been written on it with a blue marker.

"Whatever." Ron walked around Mike and opened the door to the left side of the plane. He hopped in and slammed the door. He checked his pockets for the keys but couldn't find them. Mike opened the door on the other side of the cockpit. "I have another favor to ask you."

Ron gave Mike a look that could melt a glacier. "I don't care. The answer's no."

"But I haven't even-"

Ron cut him off. "I said, no."

Mike stood there and watched Ron check his pockets again. This time he checked his back pockets, too.

"Toledo," Mike said.

"What?" Ron replied while feeling his shirt for any lumps that might be keys.

"I need a lift to Toledo."

"Not going to happen, unless you can find my invisible keys," he mumbled.

"Deal." Mike pointed. "Right there."

Ron shifted to see past the yoke. He had left the keys in the ignition. He covered his face and groaned.

"It's only about a hundred and twenty-five miles. Around an hour flight, right? Straight shot." Mike hopped in with a big smile on his face. "I apologize if I'm interrupting any vital plans for today. But this is really important."

"You said the trip here was important."

"It was."

"Well, you weren't here very long."

"Neither were you."

"I wasn't planning on landing in Zanesville."

"But aren't you glad you did? You must have gone somewhere since you weren't here when I got back."

"I went . . ." Ron shook his head. "It's none of your business."

"Aren't you curious where I went?"

"Not in the least."

"I'd like to hear where you were if you don't mind."

"I do mind. I don't feel like talking right now." Ron thought about Toledo. There was a huge lake outside that city. He could disappear in the middle of Lake Erie with barely a splash.

"You already know I'm a good listener, but only if you need an ear. Otherwise, you won't even know I'm here."

Ron glared at Mike. "Let's get this over with."

"I really appreciate this, Ron. You won't regret it. I promise."

Ron twisted the key, and the propeller tips traced the outline of a circle. The engine wouldn't start. "We might not be going anywhere."

"Don't you want to follow the checklist?"

"Do I want to follow the checklist," Ron sarcastically parroted back. "I've flown this plane for hundreds of hours. I think I know what I'm doing."

"Okay."

The result was the same when Ron tried to start the engine a second time. He reached into the map pocket and pulled out the checklist. He shook his head when he realized he hadn't pushed the mixture control forward. He did so, twisted the key and the engine came to life.

"Not a word," he said to Mike coldly.

Ron taxied the airplane along the taxiway toward the runway. "It looks like the wind's the same as before, so we'll use runway 22." He remembered to turn the radio on. It was still tuned to the local airport's traffic frequency. Knowing that another close call could end far worse than the earlier one, he positioned the Cessna at the entrance to the runway with the plane angled to give the best view of any aircraft approaching to land. After searching the local airspace for other aircraft, he picked up the mic and announced his intentions to take off. "Holler if you see another plane."

"Absolutely."

The RPM gage indicated the engine was producing full power as the plane rolled down the runway. Ron pulled back on the yoke and the Cessna broke free from the ground. As the aircraft climbed following the runway heading of southwest, the familiar fall colors that painted the southern Ohio landscape in the fall came into view below.

Mike took a deep breath. "Just beautiful, isn't it? Makes a man glad to be alive."

Ron ignored the observation and kept the airplane in the same configuration as it climbed. His thoughts drifted to Jerry's family. A twinge of guilt chipped at the wall he'd built against the world as he remembered how he left things with Sarah. He wished he'd thanked her for lunch and had been more personable before leaving.

He thought about Robert and hoped that the guy had a renewed appreciation for his position as a family man. He wished he could fill Robert with the intangible value, which came with having a family. A man shouldn't have to lose those he loves to realize what they mean to him. How could God allow such a thing?

Even with various thoughts competing for his full attention, Ron noticed Mike was glancing toward him more often. Or was Mike looking at the instrument panel. Ron scanned the panel and engine instruments for indications of anything outside of normal parameters. He became more vexed with Mike's stares. "What?"

"Is this the right way?"

"We're, uh, well . . ."

"I'm pretty sure Toledo is north or northwest."

"Can you get me the sectional? It's stuffed in the pocket behind my seat."

"Does this make me your copilot?"

"Do you want to get to Toledo?"

"Just trying to lighten things up a bit. You still seem tense."

Ron closed his eyes and shook his head. He glanced at the altimeter and saw they were passing through six thousand feet. He saw Mike unfolding the sectional chart, a navigation map that covered the northern half of Ohio. He grabbed the chart from Mike and gave it a cursory glance. "We probably need to be on a heading of around three-two-zero." Ron turned the yoke slightly to the right and the aircraft responded by slowly banking right. Once the aircraft was almost to the desired heading, he held the yoke to the left for a couple seconds, which stopped the turn. Now the plane was on a northwesterly heading.

"This direction feels right," Mike said.

"If we hold this course, we should be in Toledo in an hour or so."

"Great. Thank you, again."

"Don't mention it."

The familiar drone of the engine helped to relax Ron. For years, he had told people that one of the wonderful joys of flying small airplanes included leaving one's problems back on the ground. But today, every moment he'd experienced was a part of him that gnawed from the inside. What was Mike doing here in his airplane and what was the point of helping him? Why would a man like Robert suddenly give up when he had a family to look after? And why didn't he deny Mike this flight so he could quench the rage and pain that ate away at his soul with the one quick action that kept getting delayed? A glance out the side window replaced the questions with other thoughts.

Below, a road that disappeared under the cover of trees was another reminder of his last flight with Anne and the road that led home. Every few minutes, she had remarked how beautiful the view was. *This is what God sees every day*, she said. *Isn't this the most beautiful sight you've ever seen?* Ron remembered her smile as she absorbed the view below. *Yes, yes it is,* he said.

"You okay?" Mike asked.

"Just thinking," Ron calmly replied, disarmed of the caged hostilities he held within.

"I noticed you have headsets in the back. Would it be all right if we put them on?"

Another of Mike's seemingly endless requests, yet this was one Ron agreed with since it was relatively loud inside the plane. With the headsets plugged into the intercom, it would be much quieter. "Go ahead."

Mike unlatched his seatbelt. Ron leaned away as Mike leaned on the top of his seat with one hand while reaching for the closest headset in the back on the floor. Ron's jaw clenched in annoyance, and it occurred to him how easily he was upset every time something inconvenienced him ever since he lost his family. He had been what Anne referred to as a *tri-C personality*—cool, calm, and collected. But with his world turned upside down, even the smallest of details angered him.

Mike fell back into his seat and latched the seatbelt. He unwound the cable from one headset and handed it to Ron, and then he did the same with the second one. They both plugged the headsets into the intercom.

"Can you hear me?" Mike asked.

"Yes."

"What were you thinking about?"

Ron felt duped as he realized Mike just wanted the headsets to help facilitate conversation – yeah, should have seen that coming. "Persistent, aren't you?"

Mike glanced over and smiled.

"The foliage below reminded me of the last time my wife and I went flying together, that's all."

"How long have you been flying now?"

"I took a few lessons during college, but didn't finish until after I had graduated. It was expensive but worth every penny." Ron smiled as he reflected on old memories that weren't quite as polished as they used to be. Now, they were more like reflections off a lake, still beautiful but hazy replicas of the original.

"Financially, buying an older model Cessna like this one didn't break my budget."

"What year is she?" Mike interrupted.

"1965."

"Wow, a classic."

For the first time, Ron laughed at Mike's remark. "She didn't cost more than a decent car when I bought her, so I rationalized the purchase pretty easy. They say a pilot is often partial to the type of aircraft he learned to fly in, and I learned in a Cessna, so I wanted a high-wing. Another pilot I knew called to let me know this one was for sale, so I had it inspected and bought it."

"Is there much difference between this one and a newer one? From the outside they look about the same."

"The biggest difference is this one has the Continental six cylinder in it, and the newer ones have Lycoming fours."

"So the older ones are more powerful?"

"Actually the newer ones are by a five or ten horsepower, I think."

"Sounds like you must have some great memories after flying for what, a decade now?"

Ron became pensive when Mike said *memories*. He felt the pain pull his heartstrings as he remembered the only remnants he had of Anne and Bradley were memories.

Ron felt himself clamming up. "Don't worry about it." He always thought he knew himself and his capabilities until his family was killed. Since then, his own thoughts randomly massaged or traumatized his heart. He wished a pill existed that could delete painful memories while keeping the rest. He wanted to remember just the joyful ones.

"When Anne told me she was pregnant with Bradley, I about had a heart attack."

Mike laughed.

"We weren't really trying to have kids at the time, but we had talked about it and were open to it. We figured, just let nature take its course and whatever is meant to be, will happen.

"One morning, we were having breakfast at the table when Anne knocked her chair over in a rush to get to the bathroom. I didn't know what to think, so I ran after her. Even before I got to the bathroom, I heard her vomiting. I thought she just had a sudden case of the flu or something."

Mike nodded.

"I stood there for a few seconds when she looked up at me holding onto the toilet bowl like one of my hung-over fraternity college buddies. She looked at me and said 'I'm pregnant.' Her nose was running and tears were streaming from her eyes. She looked like something the cat dragged in. But let me tell you, I thought she was beautiful.

"I didn't believe her at first, but then she said she didn't know how to tell me and had held off on it for two weeks already because she wasn't sure how to break the news. I asked her why. She said I was working so much that she didn't want to disturb my work. Can you believe that? She was always so considerate like that. Even to the point of sacrificing her own comfort just to make other people happy."

Ron blinked rapidly as he felt tears coming. "I miss her *so* much."

Mike smiled at Ron and put his hand on his shoulder for a moment. When he removed it, Ron was relieved that Mike hadn't said anything to try and make him feel better.

That guy's learning, Ron thought.

Nearly an hour later, Mike still hadn't said anything else. Ron's head felt like it was in a haze.

"We don't have to fly over the lake, do we?"

Ron saw that Mike was pointing straight ahead. He saw the large body of water forming at the horizon. Lake Erie. Ron gasped. "I need to call Toledo approach. I hope we're not in their airspace yet."

"What happens if we're in their airspace?"

"They shoot us down with missiles," Ron sarcastically replied.

Mike folded his hands and rested them in his lap. Ron was glad Mike hadn't missed a good opportunity to shut up.

"Let me see the chart," Ron said as he pulled out the sectional and unfolded it. "I need the frequency for Toledo Approach."

Mike watched Ron adjust the radio frequency. Next, Ron held down a small button on the yoke. "Toledo approach, this is Cessna five five seven eight Mike, inbound for landing."

Mike could hear the radio chatter over the headset. "You tell them the name of your passenger when you land?"

"No, that's our call sign. Didn't you see it on the sides of the plane? 5578M, but for the M you say Mike on the radio."

"Oh, I see."

Over the headset, they heard, "Aircraft calling Toledo Approach, squawk four eight four six."

Ron cursed. "I forgot to turn the transponder on." He turned the device on and adjusted the four numbers from 1200 to 4846. "Squawk four, eight, four, six, for Cessna five, five, seven, eight, Mike."

A few seconds later they heard, "Cessna five, five, seven, eight, Mike, radar contact eight miles southwest of the airport. You are already within Toledo's class C airspace. Call the tower upon landing. And say altitude."

Ron swore a little louder. He pressed the talk button and replied that he'd call the tower upon landing. He reported the altitude as indicated on the altimeter of four thousand four hundred. "How'd we drift down over two thousand feet in the past hour?" Ron cursed again as he shook his head. "Thanks a lot, Mike."

"What did I do?"

"You just had to go to Toledo, didn't you?"

"Honestly, yes."

Ron concluded Mike was unaware of the potential consequences. Ron had never had an airspace violation before and wondered what would happen once they landed. "What in Toledo could be so important that you absolutely had to get there today?"

Over the headsets they heard, "Cessna five, five, seven, eight, Mike, left turn heading two, seven, zero, vectors to runway two, five."

"There is . . ." Mike began.

"Quiet." Ron pressed the button on the yoke. "Two, seven, zero for seven, eight, Mike."

Mike remained mute while Ron spoke with air traffic control. Over the next ten minutes, Ron changed course and descended as directed until they landed on the two mile-long runway. Ron taxied the plane and shut the engine down after parking it among other small airplanes on the general aviation ramp. He removed the key from the ignition and consciously put it in his front pocket.

"Got to call the tower," Ron mumbled.

"Anything I can do?" Mike asked.

"Yes," Ron sighed. "Leave. Just leave."

Mike opened his mouth as if to speak but didn't say anything. He unlatched the door on his side on the plane and exited.

When Ron got out, a young man wearing jeans and a bright orange vest greeted him. "Sir, I understand the tower wants to talk with you. I can take you to a phone."

Ron remembered he still had the cell phone in his pocket. He also remembered there was a message on it.

"I have my own phone. If you'd just give me the number, I'll call them later."

"You need to talk to them now."

Ron thought of hopping back in the plane and taking off. What were they going to do, cite him for another violation? If he carried out his plans, they'd have to use divers to fish him out of the lake first. He stood still in hesitation while keeping a hand on the wing strut.

"Are you all right, sir?" the man asked.

"Fine, let's go."

Ron and the lineman walked across the tarmac. Ron felt a small ripple of excitement, in spite of himself, as he walked past a small white jet with yellow stripes.

"What type of jet is that?" He asked the lineman.

"One of those VLJ aircraft."

"VLJ?"

"Very Light Jet."

"I haven't been following jets. Out of my price range."

"That makes two of us."

"What do you know about that one?"

"It belongs to Dr. Graybill. He bought it two years ago. He has a clinic here and over in Pennsylvania. I think in Pittsburgh, maybe? Anyway, he uses the jet to commute."

"Beats driving."

The lineman laughed. "Sure does."

They entered the general aviation building, and Ron followed the lineman to a small, plain room with a couple of large tables and two black, corded phones on the wall.

"Just hit nine, one for the tower."

"Sure, thanks," Ron said. He sat down and picked up the receiver. He replayed the events of the past half-hour in his head. He wanted to clock Mike in the mouth so hard the man would never speak again. He dialed the number to reach the tower, and the man who answered said James was already on his way down.

No sooner had Ron hung up the phone when a bald man who was in his 50's wearing a white shirt and navy blue pants walked in. His light blue tie had vintage World War II aircraft on it and there was a small notepad in his hand. Ron was pretty sure this was the guy.

"James?"

The man yielded a conciliatory grin and sat down across the table from Ron. "Cessna five, five, seven, eight, Mike?" The man said with a discernible British accent.

"Yes."

"Were you pilot in command?"

Ron nodded.

"What happened up there?" He voice got louder and he leaned in as he said, "You know we had to vector two commercial aircraft to maintain separation due to that stunt you pulled? Why didn't you have the transponder on?"

Ron closed his eyes and took a deep breath. He didn't want to lose his pilot license but at the same time, he knew that his conduct had been grossly unprofessional and arguably dangerous. For the first time today, he felt a new emotion: fear. He was afraid of losing his license.

"It turned out a breaker had popped," Ron lied. "Once I saw it, I realized why I wasn't getting a reply from approach. I should have noticed it sooner."

Ron saw the man surveying his face. "If it wasn't passed three already, I might just have you walk out to your plane with me so we could take a quick look at that situation. But I need to get home."

Ron breathed a sigh of relief.

James leaned back in the chair. "I checked to see if you at least got a weather briefing-"

Ron knew getting a weather briefing was required but he hadn't bothered with it. Crap. Who knew how many regulations he had broken that day?

"And I see you checked the weather for—" James glanced down the notepad. "Let's see, Zanesville, Toledo, and New York." He looked back up at Ron. "I'm sure the briefer told you about the convective activity predicted for Eastern Pennsylvania."

Ron wanted to interrupt the man, but kept his mouth shut. If Ron hadn't called for a weather briefing, who had? Mike? It had to have been Mike because who else knew he'd be at the Toledo airport today? Mike and only Mike because not even Ron knew he'd be going to Toledo until a couple hours ago. However, now at least he knew Mike was expecting him to fly him to New York. Absurd. No way was he going to let Mike take advantage again. This time he'd be ready. And it was time for Mike to answer some questions.

The FAA inspector paused. "Mr. McQuillen, are you listening?"

"What? Yes, yes, of course."

The inspector looked Ron over in a judgmental manner. "I don't think I should let you get away with what just happened. I'm going to have to take your license."

"And you're from the FAA?"

"Of course I'm from the bloody FAA."

"I never met anyone from the FAA with your accent. I apologize."

James stood up. "Just give me your license and I'll forget your xenophobic attitude. Now if you'll hurry up and surrender it, maybe I'll have the FAA Administrator suspend it just temporarily."

Ron deflated and shook his head. "Look, I messed up. It was my mistake. Can't you let it slide just once?"

"Why? Tell me, what have you ever done to deserve a second chance?"

Ron's head tilted down toward the table. He wiped his sweaty palms against his pants.

"That's what I thought. Your pilot's license, please."

Chapter 6

Einstein

Ron's jaw dropped. "Sir, I think that's a bit extreme."

James leaned toward Ron. "Extreme? You think the public wants to read about daydreaming pilots in small planes colliding with jets over cities? How's that for extreme?"

"Well, I . . ."

"Plus, you're making me late. I was supposed to be out of here at three."

Ron looked at the clock on the wall, which indicated ten after three.

"Mr. Rogers? When are we going?" A boy about ten years old in faded jeans and a white t-shirt was standing in the doorway. His black hair was slicked back like a miniature Jimmy Stewart. His left hand was covered with a baseball mitt.

James was facing away from the doorway, and he didn't turn around to face the kid. "Wait by the car. I'll be there in a minute."

"But Mr. Rogers . . ."

"Einstein! The car! Now! Or no McDonald's."

The boy groaned then kicked the plastic trashcan. It landed a few feet away from the table where the men were seated.

"Kids," James mumbled. He looked at Ron. "Would you believe he's not even mine?"

Ron shrugged with indifference. He reflected on how he had ended up in Toledo when his initial plans put him at the bottom of a small lake in the middle of nowhere.

"He belongs to our neighbor, but he often takes the bus to the airport after school. He likes airplanes. Oh, and he says that, other than his mom, I'm the only one who's nice to him."

"You?"

James laughed. "When I'm not keeping the friendly skies safe, that's my second job."

"What do you mean by 'nice to him?'"

"His dad's some hot shot lawyer in the city, a big guy with a small temper who played ball in college. Did I mention he's also my neighbor? Sometimes, the kid claims his dad hits him, but I've never seen any evidence." James looked down and frowned. "The man just yells a lot."

Ron stared at the small plastic trashcan that was on the floor nearby. It lay on its side with marks from where the kid had kicked it. Its crumpled contents were spilled all over the floor. It was how he felt: kicked, empty and crushed. Like the trashcan, some people might show damage on the outside. Ron's was still hidden.

Realizing he'd volunteered too much information, James got quiet. His fingers gently tapped the tabletop. "What's your name again?"

Ron hesitated in surprise of the topic change. "Ron. Ron McQuillen."

"That matches the same as was on the Cessna's registration. You have your license on you, Mr. McQuillen?"

"Well, I . . ."

"I can just submit an administrative action to have it suspended if you aren't going to surrender it."

Ron met James's stare with one that was equally firm. But he eventually pulled his wallet from his back pocket, removed his license, and tossed it on the table.

James took the laminated license, looked it over and tucked it into his front shirt pocket. "I'll file a report tomorrow. The FAA will contact you with their decision. You can check their website for how these things are handled."

"Anything else?"

"We're going to need to see your logbook."

Ron nearly swore, but he caught himself. He remembered the Cessna wasn't locked. "It's in the plane. What else?"

James looked behind him toward the doorway. "For you? That's it," he said without so much as glancing at Ron. He pulled a smart phone from the small pouch on his belt and tapped the screen.

The man's condescending attitude made Ron feel ever smaller. He got up and quickly exited the room. He was bewildered by the bad stroke of luck that had struck him. It was an ugly trend that seemed to have taken over his life. He cursed Mike for bringing him to this middle of nowhere.

Black and white photos from the airport's earlier days adorned the hallway, which led to the exit. Ron barely noticed them. He used to love aviation. He used to love flying. But it no longer brought him relief from his pain.

He exited the building, and the roar of a departing commuter jet filled his ears.

"I said, hey mister."

Ron looked down. The boy was sitting on the pavement, leaning against the building. A baseball mitt with the palm side down was beside him. "Hey." Ron forced a quick smile.

"You a pilot?"

A brief laughed escape his lips. "I was."

"What do you mean, you were? Did you forget how to fly? How do you forget how to fly?"

"I didn't forget. Something just came up." Ron didn't want to discuss what had happened with the FAA guy with some dumb kid, even if the kid's name was Einstein. "So why do people call you Einstein?"

"They say I'm smart." He looked down and fidgeted with a stone. "My dad says I'm just a smart-alec."

Ron recalled what James had said. "How's your dad treat you?"

The boy shrugged. "Not so good since my mom died."

"I'm sorry to hear she died."

"Actually, she didn't die. My dad just says that all the time because she left him. He says she's dead to him, whatever that means. He was mean to her, too. I wish I could leave."

"Why don't you live with your mom?"

"She doesn't have any money. She works real hard in some train car."

"A train car?"

"Yeah, you know, one of those trolleys where they serve you food and coffee and stuff."

"Oh, I see. A diner."

"Yeah. But it isn't a job where they pay you much money. She puts in lots of hours. She tells me to study hard so I don't end up like her. So I do."

"Is that why people call you Einstein? You're smart because you study hard?"

The boy flicked a rock from between his thumb and middle finger. "I guess so. But I don't feel smart. If I were smart, I'd know what to do. But every day I wake up and I want to run away, but I never do. I keep hoping someone here will show me how to fly planes. I want to be a pilot. Then I could fly away – far, far away from my dad, and he'd never yell or hurt-" Einstein abruptly stopped talking. "I just wish he'd be nice to me. That's all." He looked up at Ron. "And my real name's Bradley, not Einstein."

Ron's heart skipped a beat. For a few moments he watched Bradley pick random stones and flick them away.

"Bradley?"

"Uh-huh."

"That's a good name."

"Thanks."

The trio of the boy, his dad and James intrigued Ron. "So where does James, er, Mr. Rogers, fit into all this."

Bradley's eyes lit up. "Mr. Rogers is nice to me. He plays catch with me and lets me spend the night with Edward at their house."

"Edward?"

"Yeah, his son, Edward. So, I live with them as much as I can. Mrs. Rogers is real nice. She's like Mom, but more real because she's always there." Bradley studied Ron's face. "What's your story?"

"My story?"

"You don't need to repeat everything I say unless you're hard of hearing. Do I need to talk louder?"

Ron searched for an explanation. He knew he hadn't been thinking right all day.

"Oh, never mind." Bradley picked up his mitt and the baseball that was under it.

Ron noticed the baseball had *AM* written on it in a blue marker. "Where'd you get that ball?"

Bradley shrugged. "A guy just gave it to me?"

"Today?"

"Yeah. He saw my mitt and said, 'Where's your ball.' I said I lost it down a drain just up the road, so I didn't have a ball anymore. He tossed me this one and said, 'Now you do.'"

"I see."

"Will you toss the ball to me?"

Ron waited for an excuse to come to him. Meanwhile, another small jet roared off the runway, which reminded him that he wouldn't be piloting any airplanes in the near future. He was stuck here, in Toledo.

Ron normally wasn't one for spontaneity, but an odd thought occurred to him. "Actually, I was wondering how your mom's doing. How would you like to go see her?"

Chapter 7
Carly's Trolley

Bradley popped up like a firework. "Really? Now?"

Ron laughed. "Sure." He felt like a part of him smiled when Bradley smiled. He was torn between being happy for the boy and missing his own son. For now, the distraction was nice.

"Great, let's go. Where's your car?"

"Why don't we get a cab?"

"I know just where to get one. But I need to tell Mr. Rogers first."

"Good idea."

Bradley disappeared into the building.

Ron inhaled the warm afternoon air. The lingering aroma of recently harvested corn reminded him of the fields back home.

Home. There was a place he'd never see again. Home had been a safe place where Anne and his son had lived. There was no home anymore. A semi-truck had barreled through and left rubble where home used to be. Now Ron felt like a nomad, cursed to walk the earth ensconced in a shroud of loneliness and despair. However, today he was beginning to find that being around someone else helped him to forget his situation, so long as he didn't think.

James kicked open the door with Bradley in tow. Ron's logbook was in his other hand. "Who do you think you are?" He yelled.

"What do you mean?"

"You think you're going to disappear with Bradley? Let me tell you, Mr. McQuillen, you've got another thing coming."

Bradley jumped up and down while tugging on James's shirt. "Mr. Rogers, he's going with me to see my mom. Please let us go. Please, please, please . . ."

James lowered himself to rest on his heels and placed a hand on the boy's shoulder. "Son, we don't even know this man. You can't go running off with some stranger."

"But he doesn't feel like a stranger to me," Bradley protested.

"Tell you what," Ron said. "How about I give you my cell phone number so you can reach us anytime."

James looked at Ron with distrust and stood up. "This isn't like Bradley to run off with some stranger he just met." He crossed his arms and kept a focus on Ron. He opened Ron's logbook and started flipping through it.

Ron looked at Bradley who met his gaze with a shrug. For the next two minutes, the two of them watched James scan a page of the logbook, turn the page and scan the next one. James paused around the tenth page. He studied it intently and held it close to his eyes for a second. He flashed a smile, then remained focused on the page.

James looked at Ron. Then he looked down at Bradley who smiled at him. "What's your cell number?" He said to Ron.

Ron gave him his cell number, which James entered into his phone. He wondered what the man had spotted in his logbook. A second later, Ron's cellphone rang from his pants pocket. Bradley got up and stood beside Ron.

Convinced that he had the right number, James ended the call. "How do I know you're not some sort of nut-job who's going to kidnap Bradley? I already know you can't fly any better than a wounded bird."

Ron looked down. He noticed two lines of ants going both directions between the sidewalk cracks. He felt just as big. He looked up and directly into James's eyes. "I guess you don't. But I'm not." He remembered what Mike had said to him when they had first met earlier that day. "My word is all I can offer you."

"Ohhhh." Bradley groaned.

"Wouldn't you rather go to McDonald's?" James asked.

Bradley looked at the ground and kicked a stone. "I'd rather see my mom. Her burgers are better."

The three of them stood there while the engine noise from a small airplane filled the air. Ron reflexively angled his head up toward the sound and saw that a small Cessna similar to his was departing, except this one was white with blue and yellow stripes.

"Okay," James said to Bradley. "You can go, but I'm coming with you. We need to be at my house by dinner time."

"When's that?"

"Six o'clock."

Bradley stuck out one hand, made a fist and quickly pulled it in. "Yes," he said in victory.

"Mr. McQuillen, it takes about fifteen minutes to get to my place from the diner, so that'll give Bradley plenty of time to visit with his mom. It'll also give you and I time to discuss other matters."

"I think that's reasonable." He felt James's eyes on him, searching for a reason to deny the jaunt. He expected the man to volunteer what tidbit of information he had spotted in the logbook, which apparently had changed his attitude.

James slapped Bradley on the back. "You ready to go see your mom?"

"Yes, sir, Mr. Rogers."

"Good." He looked at Ron. "Let's go to the main terminal and I'm sure we'll find a cab."

"I'll get us a cab!" Bradley ran across the grassy field that butted against the main terminal.

"We aren't going to take your car?" Ron asked.

"Not this time," James replied.

Ron was perplexed, but he found the arrangement fair since his only concern was that Bradley spend time with his mom.

Ron and James walked toward the terminal. "I hope you can understand why I can't just let you run off with

Bradley," James said. "In my household, he's family. Only a father would know the significance of having a son."

Ron winced, but he quickly quenched the expression with a forced smile. He wanted to tell James how well he knew the truth of his words, but didn't want to pick at the fresh scar. "It's a privilege."

James nodded and slapped Ron on the back.

Ron presumed they'd talk about the logbook later. He saw that Bradley had already put a football field of distance between them and was waving at passing cabs. When a cab came too close to the boy, Ron felt a nervous rush run down his spine as he suddenly feared for Bradley's safety. "Bradley, stay on the sidewalk," he yelled. He and James increased their pace.

Bradley was hopping into a cab as they caught up with him. "In here, Mr. McQuillen," he waved.

"I'll sit in front," James said as he opened the front door and got in the passenger's seat. Ron got in the back. "Be sure to stay on the curb next time," he said to Bradley.

There was a plastic partition between the front and back seats with a slider in the middle that was open. "Where to, gents," the cabby said.

Bradley interrupted James to give the driver directions. He closed the slider. Minutes later they were driving between recently harvested cornfields.

Ron could faintly hear James and the driver making small talk. Bradley was quiet. Ron watched the boy gazing out the window. "Are we there yet?" he joked.

Bradley didn't respond. His demeanor had changed since they had left the airport.

Ron leaned forward to see the boy's expression. He saw tears running down his face. "Bradley, what's wrong?"

"She's not bad like my dad says."

"What do you mean?"

"Didn't my dad tell you she was mean and that she hit me and never bought me anything?"

"I've never spoken with your dad."

"Oh, well, that's good. He'll just fill you with lies." He sniffed a few times.

Ron noticed a small box of tissues sticking out of the map pocket of the seat in front him.

"Here." Ron passed Bradley a couple tissues.

Bradley dotted his eyes and blew his nose.

"I wish I could stay with her, but she says she can't give me what my dad can. I told her I don't care. I don't want anything."

Ron looked away from Bradley and stared out the window for a few seconds. But he didn't see anything. His eyes remained unfocused as his thoughts and empathy for the boy consumed him. He felt helpless.

"Why can't my dad just be nice to me? What did I do?" He started crying harder. "I think he punishes me sometimes just because I'm alive."

"Hey, hey. Come here." The boy leaned against Ron and sobbed. Ron put his arm around him. His own emotions tried to breach, but he fought and kept them suppressed. He wished he knew more about the situation.

Like back-to-back reruns, more harvested fields passed along with white, two-story farmhouses of various sizes. Outside, the world appeared to have everything in place as the shadows from telephone poles slowly stretched over the road and fields.

"You're really going to like my mom. Everyone does."

"I'm sure I will."

"Once you meet her, you'll see. She's the nicest mom ever."

Ron smiled. "I can't wait."

"Me neither."

Ron's cell phone rang. He pulled it out of his pocket and answered.

Bradley's nose wrinkled. "Who is it?"

"Here." Ron handed the phone to Bradley. "It's James, er, Mr. Rogers." He saw James holding a cell phone to his ear right in front of them.

Bradley took the phone. He laughed. "Yeah, we're getting there now. Just look forward . . . see you then, bye." He hung up and gave the phone back to Ron.

"What did Mr. Rogers want?"

Bradley rolled his eyes. "Just to make sure you didn't kidnap me. He was being silly." He kicked the back of the seat. From the front of the car, Mr. Rogers turned his head and flashed a quick smile.

Ron laughed as he put the phone back in his pocket.

The cab slowed for a flashing red light. A semi-truck crossed in front of them, and Ron caught himself before curse words escaped his lips. The cab rolled through the intersection and then pulled off into a gravel parking lot. It stopped in front of a diner with a pink neon light that read, *The Trolley*. The exterior was aluminum with red steps that led up to the entrance on one end. It appeared to be a former passenger train dining car. A thin cloud of dust from the disturbed gravel parking lot slowly enveloped the cab.

Bradley jumped out. "Follow me. She's in here." He ran up the four steps and disappeared inside the diner.

Ron paid the driver through the partition and got out. James's phone rang as he was stepping out.

"What?" He looked at Ron and shook his head. "Fine, I'll be there shortly." He hung up and got back in the cab. "I need to get back to the airport. Bradley's with his mom now so I know he's safe. We'll talk soon, Mr. McQuillen." He pulled the door closed. Ron watched him speak to the driver who put the car back in gear. The cab exited the dusty parking lot and disappeared behind the cloud of dust that chased it.

Standing in the open air emphasized the contrast between this area and the rolling hills of Southern Ohio. The forests near his home and Zanesville had a speckled tarp of reds, yellows, and rusty browns. Here the ubiquitous shades of earthen browns and yellows from the recent harvest prevailed. There were only three vehicles in the parking lot, all of them pickup trucks that appeared to be at least a decade old.

He climbed the steps and entered the diner. The inside was a throwback from decades earlier. The black and white, now beige, checkerboard floor was topped by a line of stools next to a counter that ran much of the length of the diner. A thin aisle behind the stools led to a pair of tables at the other end. An old man wearing a *John Deere* hat was sitting at the counter three stools from the entrance. Half-eaten pie and a cup of coffee were set in front of him. Two other men were seated at one of the tables at the far end of the diner. Judging by their clothes, Ron assumed these patrons were farmers.

Bradley was kneeling on a stool beside the man seated at the counter. He saw Ron, hopped off the stool and walked to the stool at the end of the counter. He waved for Ron to join him.

"My mom will be out any second." He pulled a menu from beside a small tabletop juke box. "Be sure to order one of the burgers. They use my mom's recipe. It should be world famous."

Ron smiled and he sat down beside Bradley. "What makes a burger world famous?"

"The fact that my mom makes it."

"Then I'll have to order one."

"And get fries, too, so I can borrow some."

"You know if you borrow something that means you're going to give it back."

"I don't think you'd want them back."

"How about I just give you some."

Bradley shrugged. "Okay." He looked past Ron toward the entrance. "Where's Mr. Rogers."

"He got called back to the airport."

Ron heard a woman's voice grow louder as she exited from the kitchen. "Who wants more coffee?"

"Mom!" Bradley hopped off the stool.

Ron guessed Bradley's mom to be around thirty-five. She had a petite build, olive skin and brown hair pulled back into a ponytail. Her mustard colored waitress uniform was adorned with a stained apron, which appeared to have had years of use. When she smiled, Ron noticed that her austere appearance was enhanced through her smile and bright but tired blue eyes. "Bradley!" She rounded the counter, set the coffee pot down and embraced her son. "It's so good so see you." They held each other like they hadn't been together in years.

The reunion caused emotions that threatened to show on Ron's face, but he managed to keep them at bay.

"Are you all right, sir?" Bradley's mom asked.

Apparently, he hadn't kept all of his emotions completely hidden. "Yeah, yeah. I'm fine. Just, uh, allergies." It felt like an excuse a teenager would give. "You know with all the crops in the area."

"Bradley, who is this man?" She asked cautiously.

"Mom, this is Mr. McQuillen. It was his idea to come see you. Wasn't that a great idea?"

"You were alone with this man?"

"He came here with me and Mr. Rogers, but Mr. Rogers got called back to the airport right when we got here."

"Uh-huh," she said slowly.

Ron could see the distrust on her face. "Ron McQuillen, ma'am. Nice to meet you."

"Pleasure." She gave him a once-over while holding onto her son. "My name's Carly."

One of her hands extended off the child's back and Ron shook it. He noticed her grip was very soft.

"Hey, Mom. Can you get Ron a burger and a plate full of fries?"

"He said your burgers are world famous." Ron hoped to rid the tension that he was feeling. He suspected Carly was feeling it, too.

"I don't know how world famous they are, but the folks around here seem to like them."

"Perfect."

Carly smiled. "Anything to drink?"

"Whatever you have is fine."

"We can do that." She rubbed Bradley's head to which he playfully protested. She grabbed the coffee pot and refilled the cups of the two men sitting at the table.

Ron forced a smile, but he found himself rapidly becoming more uncomfortable. The walls of the sardine-like train car felt like they were getting smaller. He felt a sweat break out his face. He instinctively reached into his pocket for a handkerchief but there was none. If only he'd stuffed a handful of tissues from the cab into his pocket. His breathing increased.

"Are you okay, Mr. McQuillen?" Bradley asked.

Ron focused on Bradley. He made the decision to conquer his fear as if he were recovering from a dive in his airplane. During his training with his flight instructor, he had practiced a type of recovery in which his eyes were covered while the instructor put the airplane in an attitude that resulted in an extreme angle up or pointed toward the ground. Then he'd have Ron take off the blindfold and regain control to resume normal flight. The feeling he was going through now felt like the first time he had tried to regain control of the diving plane. He didn't want to crash here either.

He only needed to keep his focus on Bradley for a couple more seconds to feel like he was regaining control. The boy reminded him so much of how he envisioned his own son when he grew to be that age.

"Yeah, I'm okay. Just hungry, that's all."

Bradley looked at him inquisitively.

Ron didn't want any questions. "How long have your mom and dad been separated?"

The curious look on Bradley's face disappeared as sadness replaced it.

"Don't know. I was little. A long time ago." His gaze alternated between Ron's face and the floor. "I'm going to go talk to Al and Ben at the table over there."

Before Ron could apologize or say anything else, Bradley had fled to join the men at the table. The kid seemed to know everyone, not that there were many people to know here.

Carly popped back out from behind the swaying kitchen door. She looked toward Ron then the table where Bradley was talking with the two men. She smiled then walked over to Ron. As if by habit, she wiped the counter between them. "So, Ron."

Ron felt awkward. He looked away from her and ran a hand through his hair. "Yeah."

"What's your story?" The back and forth motion of her hand slowed as she continued to wipe the already clean counter. "I'm sure you can understand a mother's concern when she sees her son with a strange man."

Ron nodded. He took a breath and met her gaze. Even though her words had been firm, he found something about her to be strangely alluring. It was a welcome distraction from his anxiety.

He briefly explained that his inbound flight and landing at the local airport were just part of a spontaneous leisure trip. He omitted the part about losing his license or what caused it. Telling his story only took a few minutes, and he was rather surprised when she didn't prod him for more details. It was like she knew enough and there was no reason to dig into a person's past if it wasn't relevant. He wanted to know more about her if only because the discussion would take the focus off him. "Bradley and I were talking just fine until I asked him how long you and his dad had been apart."

She recoiled like a fly had just landed on her nose. "Don't tell me you're here to ask me out."

"Oh, no, of course not. I can assure—."

"Because I don't date. I'm not interested in dating anyone at all. I don't care what you have or what you're promising, I'm not interested."

The concept of dating startled Ron, and he nearly fell off the stool. "I'm sorry. That's not my intention at all. I'm only in the area for—"

Carly put a hand on her hip and stared intently at Ron. "If I had nickel for every guy." She suddenly laughed. "I suppose I still wouldn't have that much."

They heard a call from the kitchen that a Carly special with pups was up.

"I'll be right back." Carly disappeared behind the kitchen door. It was obvious why guys had asked her out.

There was no denying that she was a very attractive woman even without her hair or makeup done. He could only imagine how much more striking she'd be when she was ready for a date.

Dating. There was something he'd never do again. The brief thought of it merely reminded him of the curse of loneliness that had come upon him, yet another reason to checkout.

His daydreaming was shattered with the sound of a plate hitting the counter as Carly placed his order in front of him. She set a full glass with a *Coca-Cola* logo beside it.

Ron expected her to once again run off as quickly as she had appeared, but instead she stood there.

"I recommend it with ketchup," she said.

"Yeah." Ron uncapped the ketchup bottle that was next to the menus and music box. He had to slap it a couple times which resulted in twice as much of the condiment as he wanted. He took a bite of the burger and nodded. "Mmmm."

Carly walked away and Ron expected she was going back to the kitchen, but instead she came around the counter and sat on the stool next to him. She glanced over toward her son. "I should apologize. I might have been a bit too defensive. I just noticed your ring. I didn't know you were married."

Ron squeezed his eyes shut. This wasn't a good time to talk about that. He swallowed hard. "I wasn't planning to hit on you, if that's what you're worried about."

"Would you believe I haven't dated since my divorce?"

"That right?"

"I'm afraid so."

"I'd ask why but it's none of my concern." He wanted to say he didn't care. Why did people need to lay their problems on him today of all days? No one had the capacity to help *him*, but he was expected to sit back with a notepad and deal with everyone else's problems.

Carly sat there while Ron ate. At every sound, every movement, he expected something to grab her attention. But she remained on the stool with occasional glances toward her son. By the time he had finished his meal, he was vexed that she was still beside him. But perhaps she was just curious about the man who walked into the diner with her son.

"Your other customers might need something."

"They'll be here for hours. They just talk about their day or the news. It's nice to have regulars who don't expect too much but tip as if you had given them everything. They just want their coffee warmed from time to time."

Ron considered his last hour. He had the urge to get a cab back to the airport. But the kid had tricked him into coming to this diner and seeing his mom. Was he trying to set them up? His head ached.

"You might be the quietest customer I've had all year."

"Sorry, I'm not much company today. Were you looking for a conversation?"

"No," she whispered.

Ron noticed her demeanor had softened and her body language was less defensive. Now the two seemed to fit better.

"Why do I suddenly find myself so comfortable with you, Mr. McQuillen?"

"Just Ron. Call me Ron."

"Yeah, I think you already said that."

"Carly, would you mind taking Bradley over to James's place. I told him I could do it, but I'm sure he wouldn't mind if you did." Ron tried to think of an excuse. He wanted to leave. "And like you said, I'm a stranger anyway."

"You're starting to feel less like one. Besides, I don't have a car."

"How do you get to work?"

"The owner lets me live in one of the trailers up the road pretty cheap."

"I see." Ron felt like he should leave her whatever he had in his wallet. A wave of sentiment passed through him. He wasn't sure if it was guilt, or pity or something else. He tried to find the right words to say. "I'm sorry about how, uh, your ex is being such a jerk."

"Everyone knows that. Makes no difference though."

"It should."

"It doesn't."

"I expect you'll find someone much better soon. You deserve better."

"I used to think so, but not anymore. Anyone better is better off without me."

"How can you say that? It's not true."

Through eyes filled with tears she looked at him as if she were about to beg. “Ron, Bradley doesn’t know this.” A few teardrops fell from her cheek as she glanced over toward the table where she heard her son’s laughter.

“Know what?”

“I’m dying.”

Chapter 8

Elise

Ron's jaw dropped but no words came out. Carly wiped away tears. He saw her hand on the counter and put his on top of it. He wanted to comfort her. She pulled her hand away and set it in her lap where the other one was holding the washrag.

"It's a tumor," she whispered.

"Can it be removed?" he whispered back. They both spoke in low tones, not wanting to draw attention to their conversation.

"Inoperable."

"I'm sorry."

"That's what everyone says."

"I mean it."

"I don't want to die."

Ron turned his head from her and looked at his empty plate. He felt like he was of no use here, but he wanted to do something to help this woman feel better before he left.

"There's no one to take care of Bradley," she said.

"Are you sure it's inoperable?"

"It's in my brain. The doctors said I have less than a year, but I guess it's hard to know for sure. I don't understand why this is happening to me." Her eyes winced with pain, which Ron tried not to feel. "What did I ever do to deserve this?"

Ron's fists clenched. "I know what you mean."

"No you don't. You can't possibly know how I feel."

"I know the feeling." He spoke slowly. "Of helplessness that comes from knowing you can't do anything for those you love most." He started to choke up.

She looked at him and saw the pain etched on his face.

"You *do* know." She reached over and grabbed his hand. "Oh Ron, I'm so sorry." He felt her squeeze his hand in reassurance as if the simple act would replace the pain. With his free hand that now trembled with fresh emotion, he rubbed his forehead.

"Your wife-"

"She's gone," he interrupted.

"Cancer?"

"Car accident. Our son, too. A semi ran the intersection."

"I don't know what to say."

He slowly shook his head as his hand ground into his forehead. "Had I known, I'd like to think that I would have told her that I loved her more often. I would have shown her how much she meant to me when we were together. I lived expecting that the promise of tomorrow would let me right any wrongs I had done today. That was a lie."

Her soft palm gently ran over his hand.

He turned to face her. "I know it sounds absurd today, but be grateful you can tell Bradley how much you love him. I never had that, and I'd give anything to get one final moment with my family to gain that sense of closure. To let them know that things will be okay because we'll all be together on the other side."

"I never thought of it that way."

"I didn't either until the time had passed."

She squeezed his hand. "I wish I knew what to say. There's no manual for this."

Ron shifted on his stool to gain access to his front pocket. He pulled a crumpled piece of paper from it. "Here."

"What's this?"

"The phone number of a . . . a friend. He's a preacher who also does some counseling. I think he might be able to help you.

He watched her copy the number onto the back of her order pad. She handed the wrinkled paper back to Ron.

"Keep it," he said.

"I think you may need it, too."

The hint of a trite laugh escaped his mouth. He took the piece of paper and shoved it back in his pocket. He hoped Jerry would be able to do more for Carly than he had for him.

There were still fries on Ron's plate, and he took a bite of one. It was tepid, but he slowly chewed it anyway. He didn't care. He could feel Carly's stare on him as he chewed. He didn't want to talk, but he didn't quite want her to leave either. But he'd prefer that she not stare.

"I know you wish that you could say goodbye," she said.

Ron swallowed.

"But, and I'm sorry if this is hard, but do you know just what you'd say to them?" Her head turned toward her son who was writing something in the newspaper that was lying on the table. The boy finished, and two men congratulated him like he had just explained Einstein's theory of general relativity.

"Every day," Ron said, "I write a new script in my head that I think is better than the one I thought of the day before. But they're all the same."

"How?"

"I tell them I love them. They say it back. We hold each other. But it's different when you know what's going to happen next."

Carly slowly ran her pen back and forth under the phone number she had copied from Ron. An already thick line of black ink became thicker. "I already know what's going to happen," she whispered.

"I wish I could have been more help."

A faint smile formed on her face. "You were." She got up and disappeared behind the kitchen door.

A few moments later, she popped out with a full coffee pot in hand. "How about some more coffee, guys?"

Carly went over to the man wearing the John Deere hat. As she started pouring, he said to only fill it halfway. She said, "Don't I always?" Ron wondered what the reasoning behind that might be. She walked down to the end of the diner.

Ron could hear her making small talk with the men at the table. When the child's laughter suddenly filled the air, it was as if all was right with the world.

The cell phone in Ron's pocket vibrated. The sensation reminded him a voice message had been left. He got up and started for the exit with the plan of listening to the message outside. But he was interrupted by the man sitting at the counter halfway to the exit.

"That was a real nice thing you done for Carly."

"Pardon?"

"Sorry, but I couldn't help but overhear your conversation. I had no idea she was in such a bad way. Rotten thing, cancer."

Ron hadn't paid the old man much attention until now. His raspy voice hinted at an ancient age. The man's blue overalls looked like they hadn't been washed in a week. His tanned arms and face resembled leather. Using both hands, the man took a sip from his cup of coffee. Ron noticed the man's hands were shaky, but he thought it best not to say anything about the observation.

"It sure ain't fair now, is it, young fellow?" he said resolutely. He slowly lowered the cup and it rattled in his hands on the counter until he released his grip.

"No."

"Well, it seems you got to her in a way no one else here ever could. I always wondered what was going on with her. I'll keep it to m'self. Ain't no one else's business but hers. Well, her and the boy's, I reckon."

"I think she'd appreciate that."

The old man slowly lifted his cup with both hands and sipped. Murmurs from behind caught Ron's attention, and he glanced over his shoulder. Carly had her back to him and was still talking with the group at the table.

"One other thing, young fellow."

"What's that?"

"Well, while you and Carly were talkin', I heard you say you wished you could tell your family how you felt."

Ron inhaled. "Yes."

"Lots of busy folks seem to say that now-a-days. It reminded me of my wife. I lost her over a decade back. But I never had those thoughts you were talkin' over."

"You didn't, why not?"

The creased edges of the man's lips formed into a smile. "Because of how I treated her every day. Oh sure, there were times when I said things I shouldn't've said and stuff like that. I suppose most folks do that from time to time. You're with one person long enough, I reckon it happens sooner or later." He turned and looked Ron in the eye. "But when Elise passed suddenly, I didn't have no regrets. I'd treated her good, and she done treated me the same way. We were just good to each other, that's all." He turned to look down at his cup on the counter and placed his hands on either side of it. "So I don't know if that kind of talk's done much for you. But I just wanted you to know. I like folks to know about her sometimes. That's all."

Ron watched the old man take another sip from his coffee cup. He was anxious to go outside and check his voice message in privacy, but he found some merit in the old timer's words. He could also see that the man just wanted someone to listen to his story. Ron reasoned he was good for at least that much, listening.

He took a few steps to leave, then stopped. He turned around and walked over to the old man. "Elise was a lucky woman. I'm glad you told me about her."

The old man looked over at Ron, and Ron could see his eyes were moist. He smiled and briefly put his gnarled and weathered hand on Ron's forearm. Ron smiled back. After a few moments, the man released his hand, and Ron finally exited the diner.

The late afternoon air felt good on Ron's face. He walked down the steps while he pulled the phone from his pocket. There was a rustic bench next to the steps, and he sat down on it. He tapped the voice mail icon on the phone's screen and held the phone to his ear.

"Mr. McQuillen, this is Sergeant Luca over at the station. You wanted to know the results of our investigation. The final report is available if you'd still like to review it. I can email or fax it to you, or you can stop by and pick up a copy. I hope you're well, Mr. McQuillen. Bye."

Ron checked his watch. It was nearly five o'clock. He called the number from which Sergeant Luca had called.

"Luca here."

"Sergeant Luca, this is Ron McQuillen."

"Mr. McQuillen, I was wondering if I'd hear back from you to today. How are you?"

Ron paused. "I've been better."

"Understandable. Mr. McQuillen, like I said in the message, the investigation is complete." He paused for a couple seconds. "You wanted a copy of the report, right?"

"Yes, please."

"I have your email address. Would you like me to email it?"

"That would be good, thanks."

"All right. I have a screen already opened and ready to send."

Ron looked around. He didn't want to read the report. He already knew what happened. A semi-truck had run a light and killed his family.

"Okay, sent. Next time you check your email, it should be there."

"Can you just tell me one thing, sergeant?"

"What do you want to know?"

"What are you charging the truck driver with?"

There was a long pause. Ron looked at the phone's screen to see if they were still connected. He held the phone to his ear. "Hello? Hello?"

"We're not."

"I'm sorry. I think I missed part of what you said. What are you charging the truck driver with?" Ron raised his voice. "He killed two people."

"Based on our investigation, Mr. McQuillen, your wife ran the light. She drove right into the path of the truck. I'm very sorry - very sorry for your loss."

Ron thought his heart stopped.

"Mr. McQuillen?"

Ron's grip on the phone loosened. It slipped out of his hand and fell onto the bench next to him. Two semi-trucks with swirling dust chasing them drove by the diner.

Your wife ran the light right into the path of the truck echoed in his head.

Ron cradled his head in his hands and lost himself in thought. It was impossible. A situation that could not possibly get worse had just gotten worse.

He heard his phone vibrating on the wood of the bench. There was nothing else the sergeant could tell him that he wanted to know. He looked down at the screen and noticed the phone number looked familiar. It vibrated two more times before Ron finally realized who it was.

"Hello."

"Mr. McQuillen?"

"Yes."

"How's Bradley doing?"

"He's, uh, he's doing well. He's talking with his mom inside the diner."

"Aren't you in the diner with them?"

"I'm just sitting outside catching some air."

"There was something I needed to take care of here, but it's done now. Can you and Bradley come back over to the airport?"

Ron rubbed his forehead. He wondered what else James could possibly do to make his life even worse. "Still at the airport?" Ron echoed.

Chapter 9

Another Chance

"Yeah. How about you and Bradley meet me back here as soon as you can."

"Sounds urgent."

"Not terribly, but there's something you need to see. You probably noticed I was going through your logbook before we left. There was something in it that caught my attention."

"What was it?"

"I'll leave you with this riddle. You've already seen it, but it was years ago."

Ron didn't reply and was only more confused. He wondered if it had something to do with a flight he had been on with his instructor. But those flights were supervised. His mind went blank. "I have no idea what you're talking about."

James laughed. "I suspected as much. Look, if I call a cab to swing by and pick you guys up, can you meet me back here."

Do I have a choice? "Okay."

"Good. Watch for the cab."

Ron ended the call and though he was curious what James was hiding, his thoughts returned to what Sergeant Luca had said. It only added to his pain that the sergeant faulted his wife, and not the other driver. How could the police allow the other driver to get away with murder? His anger needed a demon to focus on, and he knew just the icon he wanted to grind into the ground. For the first time, he wondered about the truck driver. He knew nothing about the man, assuming that it was a man. As he considered it further, he started doubting everything the sergeant had told him.

There was no closure, no justice, no reason to wake to another sunrise. Now that his plan of disappearing beneath Lake Erie's watery surface was ruled out, another plan had to be devised.

He leaned forward and rested his elbows on his knees and his chin on his fists, watching what little traffic there was. An old Chevy El Camino with a young driver blew by with the radio too loud. The blaring music was angry, but not as angry as Ron. He sifted through his thoughts for a reason not to step in front of the next semi. It had been good enough for his wife; it'd be good enough for him.

Ron rose to his feet. The gravel crunched beneath his shoes as he slowly walked toward the road. He could see a distant semi approaching, about a quarter mile down the dusty road. Everything he loved was gone, even his license to fly. Carly's situation had only depressed him more. He thought about her son. There was nothing he could do for either of them.

Ron stood at the edge of the parking lot and watched the looming semi grow larger. If he sprinted in front of it, everything would be over before the driver knew it and hit the brakes. He stared at the truck and thought of James's reaction to Bradley leaving with him to see Carly. There was something distantly familiar about the man. Had he met him before, or was it just déjà vu?

The horn from the semi blared as it rushed by. Ron coughed as dust swirled around him. He put his hands against his head and tried to capture the moment he had met James before. It left him perplexed. He turned around and walked toward the diner.

The old man wearing the John Deere cap was slowly walking down the steps. Ron caught his gaze, and the man stopped. When Ron met him at the foot of the steps, the man put his hand on Ron's shoulder. "I seen you out there by the road."

Ron looked away from the old man and up toward the diner entrance.

"Seen that look in a man's eyes before, too."

Ron remained reticent.

"In the mirror," the old man whispered. "Right after Elise passed."

"I thought you didn't have any regrets." Ron fought not to let sarcasm or envy tell the old man that he really didn't give a rip about anyone right now, including himself.

"That doesn't mean I had it easy once she was gone." Ron saw the tendons in the old man's hand strain against the skin as he gripped the railing. "I'm still here only because I choose to be. Someday it won't be up to me. But on that day long ago, it was. And it is today, too. That's all I wanted to say."

Ron's eyes darted between the entrance, the stairs and the old man's stern face. Conflicting feelings twisted within. "I need to go." He ascended the stairs and entered the diner.

Bradley was sitting next to the stool where Ron had sat. The boy was nursing a clear soft drink. A plate with remnants of a burger and fries was in front of him. He waved at Ron.

Ron walked over to him. "We need to head back to the airport."

"Why?"

"James, I mean, Mr. Rogers just called and said so."

Bradley shrugged. "Okay. But I need to tell my mom."

Ron sat down on the stool next to the boy. Carly popped out through the kitchen door. She saw Ron and Bradley and smiled at them.

"Hey Mom, Mr. Rogers called and said we need to go back to the airport."

"He's still at the airport? What's wrong? He should be back home by now."

Bradley shrugged. "I don't know. That's what Ron said."

Carly gave Ron an inquisitive look. "Is that right, Ron?"

"He said there was something he wanted to show me."

"Then why does Bradley need to go with you?"

Ron hesitated. "He doesn't. James asked that he come but if you want, I'll just tell him Bradley chose to stay here with you."

Carly looked at her son. "Bradley?"

"I was planning on spending the night with Edward." He tilted his head a bit and pleaded with her through his eyes.

Carly put her hand on her hip.

"Oh, come on, Mom, can I? Please, please, please."

Carly gave him a submissive expression. "Well, where else would you go?"

Bradley looked down. "Dad's."

"The cab should be here any minute," Ron said.

"Oh boy, another cab ride!" Bradley leapt off the stool, grabbed his mitt and baseball, and ran to the door. He opened it and was gone.

"Keep an eye on him for me, okay, Ron?"

"I'll need both of them."

Carly smiled. "Thanks for the talk earlier. I'll give that guy a call."

She walked over to him and pulled out her order pad. She wrote on it, tore the sheet off and handed it to him.

"What's this?"

"My number. I think it's a good idea that the person watching my son can reach me." Ron remembered what James had done at the airport. He pulled his cell phone out of his pocket, tapped the number she'd given him into the phone and hit *send.*

Unsure of what he was doing, Carly watched him until a low volume *Sinatra* ring tone emanated from a side pocket of her apron. She reached into her pocket and the sound stopped. "Thanks." She placed her hand on top of his for a moment and a sensation ran down his spine. It was a hauntingly familiar one he had last experienced before he was married. He put it out of his mind. A woman could never capture his love for living the way his wife had. Conflicting thoughts ravaged his tortured mind and he slowly pulled his hand back so as not to alarm Carly. She let his hand slip away. He rose from the stool, took a twenty out of his wallet, and set it on the counter with a nod.

"Thanks. It was nice meeting you, Ron McQuillen."

"You too, Miss Carly."

He exited the diner to find Bradley sitting in the open door of the cab, waving at him as if it would be hard to spot an animated boy in a cab in a nearly empty parking lot. "Come on, we're going to be late."

Ron descended the stairs with a faux sense of urgency. "What makes you say that?"

"Mr. Rogers checks his watch all the time. I don't want to get yelled at."

"Then we better get going."

Ron gave the cabby their destination and the cab was soon on route to the airport.

The familiar landscape passed by the window like a silent movie. The quiet inside the cab was enhanced by the boy's lack of words. Ron looked over at Bradley who was watching the farms roll by. Ron was grateful the boy wasn't crying this time. He looked happy, still basking in the afterglow of seeing his mom. Ron wondered what James had planned.

The cab stopped in front of the general aviation building. Bradley jumped out and ran inside. Ron paid the cabby and traced Bradley's path to the front door. He welcomed the sounds of the aircraft which enticed him to wait outside instead of entering. A middle-aged man wearing a white polo shirt with a yellow fancy script embroidered "G" approached the door. He was carrying a black leather case. The man thanked Ron who opened the door for him. "Strangers sure are nice folk today," he said as he smiled at Ron and walked inside. Ron thought the remark was a bit odd.

As the door was closing, it was pressed opened again and Bradley emerged. "Hey, Mr. McQuillen, want to throw the ball to me?"

The sound from a small airplane taking off reminded him that he wouldn't be piloting any airplanes in the near future. He was stuck here. A distraction from that reality was most welcome. "Sure, kid."

Bradley's eyes lit up in surprise as if he had expected the opposite answer. "All right! Follow me over here." He ran toward a field beside the parking lot. He glanced behind him. "Come on, let's go!"

Ron walked toward the field. Through clouds that looked like giant purple quills, the evening sunset did its best to brighten his countenance. He stepped onto the grass as Bradley yelled for him to watch out. He saw the ball coming at him and instinctively positioned his hands to catch it. The impact from the ball stung, but he kept hold. The kid had a good arm. Ron smiled as he threw the ball back underhanded. "Nice throw."

Bradley caught the ball with his mitt as if he had caught a million throws before. "Put some muscle into it, man," he hollered as he whipped the ball back.

The physical movement helped to loosen Ron's body, which welcomed the exercise. He caught the ball with his hands, which stung once again. Bradley had thrown the ball harder that time.

"Start running, kid. This one's going to have some distance."

"All right!" Bradley exclaimed. "Let's see what you got, mister." He started running, and the distance between the two of them grew.

Ron threw the ball high and long toward Bradley, and it looked like it would go over his head. But the kid increased his pace and dove to catch the ball. Ron couldn't see if he had it until Bradley got up and showed his glove with the ball in it. Bradley was rubbing his shoulder with his free hand as he walked toward Ron.

"Nice throw. I think I hurt my shoulder on that catch."

"Then let's go in and get some ice."

"Nah, I'm fine. Ice is for girls."

Ron laughed. He and Bradley walked toward the entrance. He looked down at the kid and reflected on the loss of his own son. The thought stung far worse than catching a ball bare handed. For an instant he wished that he could adopt Bradley, as if that would fill the void he had inside.

When they were a few steps from the door, James came out. Ron noticed that James was holding his logbook. What other damage was this man going to do, impound his Cessna?

James saw Bradley brushing at the grass stains on his shirt. "Hey, what happened?" He knelt in front in Bradley. "Are you okay?"

"We were just playing ball and I, uh . . ."

"He made a great catch," Ron said.

James stood up. "Good for you, son. Can you wait out here while I talk to Mr. McQuillen inside?"

"Awe, come on," Bradley groaned.

"It won't take but a minute," James said. He looked at Ron. "Let's go inside."

Ron followed James back to the room where he had surrendered his license. They sat down, and he felt James looking him over as if he was being evaluated.

"I went through your logbook," James finally said.

"I saw you doing that before we left to see Bradley's mom."

James set the small, black, hardcover book on the table. He opened it and quickly flipped past the first pages. Ron saw him stop at the point after Ron had been certified to fly solo as a student pilot. James put his finger next to an entry. "This was over a decade ago."

Ron nodded. "I was student pilot back then. What else are you going to cite me for?"

James ignored the snide remark. He rotated the logbook so Ron could read it. "See that entry? Look whose name that is."

Ron read the name aloud. "James P. Rogers. So?"

James laughed. "And look at the airport where you landed."

"Toledo." Ron felt dense as he put the two together. "That was you who signed my logbook?"

"Sure was. I see you were working on your solo cross-country legs and needed someone to sign your logbook when you landed to prove you were there, remember?"

"Sounds familiar."

James put his finger next to his signature in the logbook. "See the dot within both of the *E*s in my name there?"

Ron squinted and noticed that there was a single dot within both of the *E*s in the signature James had signed over a decade ago. "So what's that mean, you take my license the next time you see me?"

James shook his head. "Quite the contrary. It means that when you arrived that day, you had done so with the professionalism that comes with becoming an excellent pilot. That means that today something must have happened to distract you."

"It's been a rough month."

James searched Ron's face for more details. "Mr. McQuillen, can you assure me that what I saw today won't happen again?"

Ron put two and two together. Was this guy offering to return his license? The phrase *carpe diem* ran through his head.

"I'll be sure to go by the book."

"And?"

"And what you saw today won't happen again."

Ron watched James flip to the most recent entry on his logbook and initial the lower right corner. James put a slash mark through his initials. He closed the book and handed it to Ron. "I believe in second chances, Mr. McQuillen. Sometimes a man mistakenly does something that he wouldn't have done if he were thinking straight. Are you familiar with the practice some pilots have of leaving their problems on the ground?"

"Yes," Ron replied. In theory, the concept was sound, but he wondered how a man could forget a problem that festered in his very soul. Something like that didn't stay on the ground, it stayed with you, entrenched inside.

"I know it's personal, but might that be a practice you'd use from now on?"

Ron nodded as he ran his forefinger up and down the edge of his logbook. He nearly tuned James's presence out until he saw his pilot's license lying next to his logbook.

"You can have this back."

"Thank you." Ron looked toward the entrance just as Bradley was running past. The thought of never seeing his own son again scraped at raw wounds inside that reminded him of why he had made the decision he did that morning. It was time to go, and this time, no matter what, no Mike. Ron got up to leave. He grabbed his license and tucked it into his logbook.

James thrust his hand out. "You take care now, Mr. McQuillen."

Ron reluctantly shook his hand.

"Are you okay?"

"Yeah, yeah, um . . ."

"Just a little emotional right now, I see. That's okay. Many of us who love flying get that way about it. Welcome back."

Ron flashed a smile. "Thanks. It's time for me to go home."

"Be safe."

Ron quickly exited the room, walked through the glass-walled lobby, and out onto the tarmac. As he paced toward where he'd left his airplane, he wished he'd said goodbye to Bradley. There was a twin-engine, low-wing aircraft blocking his view of it. It was similar to the one Jerry had landed in but with blue stripes. "You better not be there, Mike," he whispered. He noticed the distinct white and yellow jet was gone. Must be nice to have your own jet. But even that luxury wouldn't salvage his family. His looked around and found that neither the beauty of the machines or the soft fields gave him any relief or hope. His desire to fill his emptiness had only one solution.

He rounded the twin-engine airplane and saw his own. There was no one standing next to it.

Now, he could follow through with what he had to do. Finally.

Chapter 10

The Dive

Ron opened the left-side door to the airplane and tossed his logbook in the foot well of the other side. He got in, slammed the door shut and pulled out the sectional chart to get the radio frequencies he'd need for the flight.

This time, he remembered where he'd left the ignition key. He went through the checklist, and the engine came to life with a twist of the key. The airplane was parked facing west, and he had to squint as he looked past the cowling and spinning propeller toward the sun, which would be swallowed by the horizon within a couple hours. He had plans to disappear below the horizon as well. As he saw it, he was going home to Anne and their son.

He radioed the tower and stated his intentions to fly on an easterly heading toward the lakeshore. The ground controller gave him departure instructions, and he dialed the assigned squawk code into the transponder. He did everything by the book, as he had promised to James.

He taxied the Cessna to the entrance of the runway and quickly ran through the pre-takeoff checklist. Once cleared for takeoff, he rolled onto the runway and applied full power. The airplane's speed increased, and Ron saw the arrow on the airspeed indicator come alive—40 knots, 50 knots, 60 knots. He gave the yoke back pressure, and the small airplane settled into an 85 knot climb while gaining altitude at the rate of 700 feet per minute.

"I'm coming home, Anne," he said. A minute later, he acknowledged the tower controller's instructions to change to the departure frequency. He looked to the north, over the city of Toledo. Everything below looked quiet and peaceful. Nothing bad that ever happened could be seen from this perspective. He thought about James's reminder to leave problems back on the ground. Back home, Ron had stated as much to fellow pilots around the airport over the years. Only after the loss of his family did he find that advice worthless.

Ron pulled the chart from the map pocket and checked his position. He saw that he was outside of Toledo's airspace, so he radioed the air traffic controller and requested a release so he would no longer be under their control. Ahead, he saw the lakeshore.

He turned the airplane to the left and established a northeasterly heading. He slowly blinked and thought about the day. There was a part of him that wanted to live, but he could find no compelling reason to do so. A life alone wasn't worth living. He replayed his time with Jerry's family and brother. He hoped he had made a positive difference in the man's life. He thought about Carly and how she had received such a rotten deal in life.

The thought of Bradley's smiling face brought a brief smile to his own. His hand still stung a little from catching the ball.

A few minutes later, he looked below to see the land disappearing into the unyielding water of Lake Erie. The water looked as smooth as glass, but as hard as his life. A few boats were scattered about, mostly within a mile of shore. It crossed his mind that many of the fishermen out on the lake below might be running away from their problems as well.

The altimeter indicated four thousand feet, plenty of altitude to put the plane into a dive and disappear in a watery splash. Hitting the water would be like slamming into concrete. His pain would be over instantly, and he would be reunited with his family. In that, he found solace.

Let's do this. He abruptly pushed the yoke forward and the negative G-forces tried to pull him out of his seat and push him against the top of the airplane. His seatbelt kept him in place. But from the back of the plane, he heard everything that wasn't tied down hit the ceiling, including the sound of the wind getting knocked out of a small boy.

"Ouch. What's going on?" yelled Bradley.

Ron turned his head from the view of the lake's surface, which now filled the windscreen, toward the backseat. He saw Bradley contorted so that the boy's head was on the floor and his legs on the seat.

Ron swore. He pulled up to take the airplane out of the dive.

"What do you think you're doing?" He yelled over the wind noise.

Bradley crawled onto the backseat. "I'm coming with you. I'm running away."

"You're being a stow-away!" Ron yelled.

The boy started crying. "I just want to get away from Dad. Don't make me go back. I'll do anything. I'll do all the chores around your house. I'll wash your plane. I'll even learn to make food. Please don't make me go back. Please, Mr. McQuillen. Please, please, please."

"We need to go back to Mr. Rogers."

"But . . ."

"We're going back to the airport. No arguments."

Over the wind noise, Ron faintly heard, "Yes, sir."

Ron put the airplane in a gradual climb to regain an altitude of four thousand feet. He turned south, and the lakeshore was visible ahead.

"Can I sit up front with you?"

Ron wished he could strap a parachute on the kid and kick him out. His plans were ruined yet again by circumstances outside his control. "Fine," he said in frustration.

"Oh boy!" Ron could hear the change in Bradley's voice, which was suddenly cheerful as if the past had been forgotten. He wished he could bounce back as resiliently as the kid.

Bradley climbed over the copilot's seat then tumbled head first into the seat. One of his shoes hit Ron on the side of the head while the other shoe hit the copilot's yoke.

"Watch it, would you? And put your seat belt on."

"Yes, sir, Captain, sir," Bradley said as he saluted.

Ron ignored the kid's theatrics. "Just what do you think you were doing? Your mom and Mr. Rogers would wonder what happened if you disappeared."

"I can't see over the dashboard," Bradley said.

"It's called an instrument panel."

Bradley looked down on either side of the seat. "Where's the button to make the seat go higher?"

"The seat doesn't go higher. It's made for adults."

"The front seat in Mr. Rogers' car goes up when you press the button. My dad's, too."

"This isn't a car."

Bradley looked at Ron with a disgusted face. "I think I know that."

From the corner of his eye, Ron saw Bradley looking around for something else.

"Where's the button for the window?"

Ron shook his head. "We don't have one of those either."

"Wow, you really got the base model, didn't you," Bradley said dryly.

"I got the . . . don't you worry which model I got. This is an excellent plane."

"Yeah, a base model plane with no power buttons."

Ron didn't reply.

"Who's Anne?"

Ron looked at the boy. "How do you know that name?"

"You said you were coming home to her right after you took off."

Ron recalled he had said something to that effect. "I thought I was alone."

"Is she your wife?"

"She was."

Bradley looked down at his lap where he fidgeted with his fingers. "You're divorced."

"No, she's just, we're . . . I'm not going to talk about it with you. Be quiet."

"Because if you're not married, then can me and my mom live with you?" Bradley became more excited. "Like I said, I'll learn how to make food, and my mom can bring it to you. You saw her at the diner. She's really good at bringing people food they like."

Ron gave Bradley a firm look. "I said be quiet. I need to talk to the tower so we can land."

Bradley tilted his head to the side and looked at Ron as if he wasn't sure he believed him, but he didn't say anything more.

Ron radioed the tower and stated he was inbound for landing. Ten minutes later, the Cessna touched down and taxied back to the general aviation ramp.

Chapter 11
Dinner

As soon as Ron shut the engine down, Bradley unlatched the door and hopped out.

"Where are you going?" Ron asked. "I bet Mr. Rogers is looking for you." He saw Bradley scanning the airfield like a prisoner calculating a jailbreak.

"I don't want to go back," Bradley hollered through the open door.

"I thought you were spending the night at Mr. Rogers's house with his son."

The boy shut the airplane door and walked around the front of the airplane as Ron got out.

"That's just tonight. Tomorrow, I'll have to go back to my dad's."

Ron clenched his jaw in frustration. There was nothing he could do about the situation. "For now, we need to find Mr. Rogers. Follow me."

Ron walked toward the general aviation building. He looked behind him to be sure Bradley was following.

But the boy had slumped beside the plane. He was sitting on the ground with his back against the wing spare. It didn't look very comfortable.

"Bradley, come here."

Bradley remained by the plane in defiance.

"If you were my kid-"

"You'd scream at me and tell me how worthless I am and how you wish I'd never been born?" Bradley interrupted with tears in his eyes.

Ron walked over to the boy and squatted down beside him. "Never. I'd never do that."

"That's why I want to go with you. I know you'd be nice to me." As tears fell, Bradley pled with Ron. "You could adopt me. And my mom, too. Isn't that a great idea?"

Ron shook his head. "You belong here."

Bradley looked down and flicked at a small stone. "I don't feel like I do."

"I wish there was something I could do for you." Ron hesitated. "Look, I'll have a talk with Mr. Rogers."

"He won't do anything."

"I don't know about that. Let me find out first, okay?"

"I already know what's going to happen."

Ron sat on the tarmac beside Bradley. "I know it's hard being a kid sometimes."

Bradley ignored him and fidgeted with his fingers. "No one loves me."

"That's not true at all. What about your mom? She loves you, right?"

He nodded. "Yeah."

"And from what I've seen of Mr. Rogers, he cares about you, doesn't he?"

The boy shrugged. "I guess."

"Let me tell you something else. *I* care about what happens to you."

Bradley looked up at Ron with puppy dog eyes. "Then why'd you bring me back here?"

"Because you belong where you can be close to your mom and those who care about you."

"But you said you care about me."

"I do. But can you picture how devastated your mom would be if you disappeared with a strange man you'd only known for a few hours?"

"I don't think you're strange. You fly crazy in a cheap plane with no power options, but I can live with that," he smiled.

Ron wasn't sure how to take the remark. "What I'm saying is that you belong here and it isn't my place to change that. Your mom would agree you belong where she can see you frequently, right? So that means living in the same area."

"I guess so." Defeated, Bradley sighed.

Ron stood up and reached for the kid. Bradley took his hand and Ron pulled him up. They slowly walked toward the general aviation building. As they neared it, Ron spotted James sitting in the lounge. He was talking on his cell phone.

Ron pulled the door open, and Bradley walked in. Ron followed. James glanced up, said something abrupt into his cell phone and put it in his pocket.

"Bradley! Where have you been?" James got up and ran toward them.

The boy remained beside Ron.

"Would you believe he tried to stow away in the back of my Cessna?"

"What?"

"I was halfway to, well, I heard something in the back and saw him. So I turned around. I knew you'd be looking for him."

James knelt and hugged Bradley. The boy looked up at Ron and rolled his eyes.

"Bradley, what were you thinking?" James asked.

"I don't know."

James glanced up at Ron then back down to Bradley. "Edward is waiting for you. And we're going to have a wonderful dinner, too." He held the boy at arm's length and waited for a response.

"Can Mr. McQuillen have dinner with us?"

Ron could see James was surprised by the question.

"Oh, uh, sure. He sure can." James stood up. "Would you care to join us?"

"And he can come swimming, too!" Bradley said. He looked up at Ron. "You can swim, can't you, Mr. McQuillen?"

"Would you believe I was a lifeguard back in college?"

"Oh boy! Did you hear that, Mr. Rogers? Can he swim with us? He can come and we'll wait an hour after dinner, and then we'll go swimming."

James sighed. "I'm afraid it's going to be too chilly tonight for swimming."

Ron rubbed the boy's hair and smiled. "Thank you for asking, but I should be going."

"Are you sure?"

Ron nodded. He looked at James and his face took on a more serious demeanor. "But there is something else I'd like to discuss with you."

"Son, go wait outside. I'll be out in a couple minutes," James said to Bradley.

Bradley slowly trudged out of the lobby toward the parking lot. Both men watched him leave.

"Mr. Rogers, I'll get straight to the point. Based on what he's been saying today, I think Bradley's dad is abusive. He might be physically abusive."

"Ah, this conversation again."

"Again?"

"Yes. In all honesty, I don't think that's the case."

"How can you say that?"

"His dad can be a real jerk, I'll give you that. And he believes in firm punishments, but I've never seen any evidence of physical abuse."

"Are you sure you're looking?"

"The boys go swimming during the summer in my pool. I've never seen any signs that Bradley's been hit."

"Hmm."

"I see you're concerned. You'd make a good father, Mr. McQuillen. Bradley's had a rough time since his parents split and even though I don't care for his dad, I haven't seen anything out of the ordinary. Like I said, this has come up before. It's good to see that people are willing to get involved and help out, so again, thank you. But I don't think things are as bad as the boy claims."

"I'm not sure I'm convinced."

James put his hand on Ron's shoulder and smiled. "You're a good man. I knew you deserved a second chance. Your attention to detail and situational awareness help to prove I've done the right thing by giving you your license back."

Ron stared out the large glass windows as a commuter jet was landing. The noise from its engines increased as the reverse thrust helped it to slow. A minute later, it was taxiing toward the main terminal at a leisurely pace.

"Is there anything else, Mr. McQuillen?"

"No, and call me Ron."

James smiled again. "Okay, Ron. After everything's been said and done, I can honestly say it's been nice to meet you." He stuck his hand out, and Ron shook it. James gave Ron a pat on the back and exited the lobby. Ron heard a squeak from the door as James exited and exchanged a quick greeting with someone entering. He could hear the murmur of the two men talking, but couldn't hear what they were saying. The conversation lasted for less than a minute.

Ron walked a few steps and stood in front of the window overlooking the tarmac and runways. He thought about the boy and prayed that he had done the right thing by not getting more involved. He felt he hadn't done anything to help the kid. He felt useless. Once he achieved the goal he'd made for himself that morning, the world wouldn't miss him anyway.

He stared at his Cessna and its long shadow. There was nothing else for him here in Toledo. It was time to go. He felt a hand slap his back.

"Glad to see you waited for me."

Ron turned around. His eyes widened.

"Mike?"

Chapter 12

Helen

Mike beamed. "Hasn't this been a great day?"

"Mike?" Ron didn't want to believe his eyes.

Mike laughed. "Isn't this perfect? I saw you coming in to land when I was looking out from the main terminal. I thought I'd come over to say goodbye."

Conflicting feelings permeated Ron's head. But he was glad to hear *goodbye* in Mike's words. "Where are you going?"

"New York."

"New York City?" Ron remembered what James had said during the interrogation.

"Yup."

"Which airport?"

"LaGuardia."

"I'm not taking you. Let's be clear about that." He was ready for a fight.

"You've already been an incredible help today, and I'm eternally grateful."

"Yeah, right. Don't mention it." No argument? He was sure Mike was going to insist. He turned to face the tarmac again. "When's your flight leave?"

"In about 90 minutes."

"You better get going. Security may take a while."

"The line only had a few people passing through, and I don't have any bags. I doubt it takes but a few minutes."

"You never know. A bus could drop off a group." He wondered why Mike didn't insist Ron fly him this time. Had Mike checked the weather? Were there storms that would prevent a small plane from flying?

Mike laughed. "I'm not too worried about that. The six thirty flight is the last one out tonight."

Ron thought for a moment. "What airport are you going through?"

"Chicago."

Neither one said anything else for the next few minutes. Ron stared out the window. The urge to escape was overwhelming. He waited for Mike to leave, but the seconds felt like hours. He was also deafly curious why Mike suddenly decided to continue without him. No matter. He just wanted the guy to leave forever. New York would be far enough.

He was glad they never exchanged addresses. Then it occurred to him that Mike could look him up through the registration number on his plane. But that wouldn't be an issue, given his immediate plans. Still, he had noticed a trend of Mike's ability to be a step ahead of things. It was like the man just *knew*.

He wanted to question Mike the way the FAA inspector had interrogated him. Then again, to just be rid of the guy would be enough.

It would be dark in a few hours. What better time to slip beneath the surface of the lake? Ron's lips pursed as he thought the concept through. Finally, something that couldn't fail. He pensively pondered it as he followed the path of a lone bird that was flying across the tarmac. It disappeared behind a hanger.

"Yup. The Windy City."

Ron found the interruption annoying. He shook his head. "What are you talking about?"

"The connecting flight is through Chicago, you know, the wind-."

"Yeah, I heard you the first time." Ron sighed. "Have a good flight. Now please leave me alone." Ron's gaze remained on the tarmac. Then two small, white butterflies fluttered about the outside glass as they tested the window. They reminded Ron of two people who were meant to be together as they flew through life facing every jagged turn as one. No matter which way they turned, they were together. Suddenly, a spider web ensnared one of the butterflies. The other flew around it. A few moments later, it, too, was caught. Ron turned away when he saw the spider coming out of its hole.

"I wanted to apologize," Mike said.

"Mike, I told you already. I need to go. Leave. Please."

"I can't."

"Of course you can."

"No, I can't." Mike sat down on one of the black leather chairs in the lounge.

Ron walked over to Mike with the intention of picking him up and carrying him to the terminal if he had to. There was only so much he could deal with in a single day, especially this one.

He stopped when he saw that Mike was getting emotional.

This was new.

Throughout the day, the man had always been upbeat, agreeable and easy to get along with. Ron hadn't been curious about the details of Mike's life, but now—.

The show of emotion made the counselor in Ron want to sit down and talk to find out what the problem was. Except this was Mike, the unwelcome passenger who wouldn't leave him alone.

The sentiment on Mike's face resonated within Ron. It always hurt him to see other people hurting. He sat in the chair next to Mike.

Ron didn't speak. He figured Mike would open up, but the silence in the lounge remained undisturbed. For the first time, Ron wondered what Mike's story was. Where was the guy before their chance meeting that morning? It was a *chance* meeting, right? Serendipity or synchronicity—Ron refused to believe it could be anything *but* that.

Mike pulled a handkerchief from his front pocket, wiped his eyes then turned to face Ron. "Have you ever done something so awful, you knew nothing could ever make it right?"

Ron swallowed hard. He wondered if Mike was running from something. He hoped he wasn't abetting a fugitive. Part of him wanted to run. Part of him wanted to witness the slow motion crash that he expected to unfold. "No."

Mike slowly shook his head. "No, of course you haven't. I didn't think you had." He fell silent.

"Have you?" Ron glanced over to the door that led outside. He also considered the hallway that led to the parking lot. He felt like he may need to run. His face flushed and his breathing increased.

"No." Mike was oblivious to Ron's inner turmoil. A smile flashed on Mike's face. He shook his head. "But there are days when I feel like I have."

Ron leaned forward and ran a hand through his hair. "Well, that's good. I mean, that's good that you haven't done anything that bad." He felt awkward.

"I'm going to tell you something that I don't share with many people. In spite of how you may feel about me right now, I think it's the right thing to do."

Ron fought the urge to run out of the room. The last thing he needed was someone else's problems to compound his own.

"Two years ago, my brother killed my wife, Helen."

Ron's jaw dropped. He looked at Mike in disbelief.

"It's true."

"I, uh . . ." Ron shook his head. "I'm so sorry."

"The anger I felt toward him was more intense than the pain of losing her. In the months that followed, it was like carrying a sack of rocks all day, every day." He glanced about the room for answers. "But he's my brother, so I still tried to help him. He's locked up in—."

"Why are you telling me this?"

"Because I want you to know I have some idea of how you hurt." Mike put his hand over his chest. "I've been there."

Ron's face filled with ire. He stood up. "How dare you say that to me. How dare you!"

Mike remained seated. "We all deal with loss, Ron. The circumstances are different, but it's still something that happens."

"Losing my family was *not* just something that happens."

"That's not what I mean. I mean, yes, it's significant. It's something with enormous weight that crushes us. But still, it's an event that happens in everyone's life. Big things tend to happen suddenly. Sometimes we get warning and sometimes not. I didn't get one. And neither did you."

Ron rubbed the base of his palms against his forehead. He sat back down and crossed his arms in a defensive posture. He nodded quickly. "I know what you're trying to do." His voice rose. "But if you're trying to be a friend, then remember how it felt when the wounds were fresh. Think back to when every breath tasted like a remnant of death laughing at you, that laughed while you suffered. You remember that?"

Mike got up. "I do. Some days the feelings are there as if they'd never left."

Ron closed his eyes as his head bowed down. "As bad as it is during the day, it always gets worse at night. Every night when I try to go to sleep, memories that I should cherish come back to haunt me."

"I know. Please believe me, I know too well."

Ron's head rose as he opened his eyes. He watched Mike's body language and believed the man was being honest. He didn't believe that anyone could feel pain as bad as he did. It was a pain personal and intimate, awful. No one should feel this.

"Why'd your brother do it?"

Mike exhaled a quick laugh. "Fear."

"Fear?"

"He was afraid she'd leave."

Ron's brow furled. "They were having an affair?"

"No. We were planning on moving out of the state. We lived in New York City, and my brother was far more than just socially awkward. My wife was always respectful and nice to him, so when he found out we were moving he just lost it. It happened while I was at work. I remember getting a call while at my desk then I got a second, more frantic call on the way home. I was in a city surrounded by millions of people, but I had never felt so alone in my life. To me, that trip back to our apartment took a lifetime."

Mike sat back down. "Traffic was a nightmare. As soon as I reached the entrance to the building, I got out and ran up the flights of stairs up to our floor. The police wouldn't let me in. I was screaming with them to let me see her, but they wouldn't let me in my own place. They had the area taped off with yellow tape while detectives were questioning my brother, Larry. I could see him seated on the couch and I was screaming at him, 'Larry what did you do, what did you do?' He looked at me with the expression of a kid who had just lost his puppy.

"I don't think I slept at all that weekend. My wife's sister, Naomi, was there and she screamed at everyone, but especially me. She kept saying how she had warned us to keep our distance from him. I guess she thought he always acted strange around her. I had never really paid any attention. I should have."

Ron's face filled with empathy. In the loss they had both experienced, he was feeling a connection with Mike, and he hated it. "Why are you telling me all this?"

"Because sometimes you can't see it coming."

"But in your case, you said there were signs."

"I didn't see them."

"I had no signs."

"I know."

Ron thought while Mike stared into space. He was starting to appreciate why Mike had offered to listen to him earlier that day. He also realized he had only volunteered a small part of his story because he wanted to keep his pain hidden. It was a type of pain that should die with him. There was nothing to be gained in the world by spreading that much hurt. He understood that Mike, too, had carried a similar pain. He wondered if it was worse when someone you knew committed the atrocity. He found that his resentment toward Mike was starting to evaporate, and it surprised him how right it felt to let it go.

"Mike, I'm sorry. I'm sorry for both of us. What did we ever do to get cursed like this?"

Mike shook his head while he focused on nothing in particular. "I wish I knew."

"I wish I could make it die, but it will only die when I do. When I had Anne and my son, I only wanted more time - more time to spend with them and to live. Now, all I have is time, and I hate every second."

"Would you believe that I really do know how you feel?"

"I'm starting to believe you do."

Mike smiled. "Of all the things to have in common, this is the worst."

Ron slowly nodded.

"But I feel like you've become a friend. Even if you don't think so, I do."

Ron saw a moth bump against the inside window. He didn't like Mike's comment. He wasn't looking for a friend, but he didn't want to come across as resentful. "I think you've got a plane to catch."

"I suppose so." He paused. "I'm going to ask you another favor."

Ron surprised himself when he didn't refuse, as if doing so thus far had been his only reflex to Mike's requests. He met Mike's gaze with raised eyebrows.

"Would you come with me to New York?"

"What?"

"Please. Come with me to New York City."

"I don't think so. Besides, we'd have to see if there were any seats left—."

Mike cut him off. "I bought two tickets."

Chapter 13

New York

"Two tickets to New York? Why?"

Mike took a deep breath. For the first time, Ron saw signs of anxiety and stress on Mike's face. Mike was becoming more human and more like him. Mike was another flawed man who was muddling through undeserved situations that were thrust upon him. "I'm going to see Helen's sister, Naomi. She's always hated me because of what happened to Helen. To this day, she still blames me."

"So you're going so that you can make yourself feel better," Ron said in a manner of fact tone.

"I want to help *her* feel better."

"What do you mean?"

"Holding that kind of resentment is no way to live. It feeds on you from the inside. It eats away at your soul and leaves scars that never heal."

"I'm not sure what you think I can do." Ron wasn't sure what to make of the assessment, but he didn't argue.

"It'd be nice to have a friend with me for support. And an objective perspective might help Naomi."

"You expect me to counsel her?"

Mike cringed. "No, not at all. I just think that, with your background, you might, uh, help point me, or her . . ." His jaw clenched as he looked down for a moment. "I think having a friend there could only help. That's all I'm asking. Nothing more."

The noise of a landing commuter jet caught Ron's attention. He concluded it was probably the same jet that would take Mike to Chicago.

"All expenses paid."

Ron looked through the window in anticipation that the commuter jet would taxi by shortly. "My airplane's parked right outside. To be honest, I'd rather just fly home."

"I'll see to it you make it back here. Your plane isn't going anywhere without you, is it?"

"It's been a long day."

"You can sleep on the plane."

"It'll be too short a flight for that."

"I would really like a friend to be with me during this." Mike sighed. "But you don't owe me anything, so you don't have to go."

"I'm sorry, Mike. But there's nothing for me there."

"What is there for you here?"

Ron shrugged.

Mike forced a smile. "I think you're out of excuses."

Ron watched the commuter jet taxi toward the terminal. He thought about Naomi, but questioned

Mike's judgment. It sounded like Naomi had been right about Larry. But the more he pondered the situation, the more he wondered if he might be able to help her, at least in some small way.

"Great," Mike said. "Let's go."

"What? I didn't say anything."

"Your face did." Mike got up and started for the hallway that led to the exit. He stopped by the hallway and turned toward Ron. "Please, Ron. I can see you know how much this means to me."

Ron looked away and remained seated. He was uncomfortable having someone assess him.

"I'll even pay you for your time. We can make it a business arrangement if you'd prefer."

To Ron, the offer sounded desperate. His morbid curiosity made him wonder what Mike would do if he refused. He saw Mike smile as he got up, but the smile faded as Ron walked toward the exit to the tarmac where his plane was parked.

"Good luck, Mike."

"I said I'd pay you."

"I don't want your money."

"What do you want?"

"Peace. I just want peace. Can you lie to me and offer me that?"

Mike was quiet. He looked down.

Ron set his hand on the handle of the door to the tarmac.

"I'm sorry, but no. I'm afraid that isn't mine to give."

Ron nodded. "Have a safe trip." He stood by the door as Mike walked down the hall and exited the building.

Ron saw Mike standing in the line of the terminal waiting to pass through security. There were only four people in front of him.

"Glad I caught up with you." He laughed when he saw the expression of surprise on Mike's face.

"I didn't expect . . ."

Ron shrugged. "I'll come along if the offer's still good."

"Absolutely." Mike nodded. He stuck his hand out and Ron shook it. "Glad you decided to come. What changed your mind?"

Ron squinted at Mike. "I can't put my finger on the exact reason. But I felt like you were being completely open with me. I appreciated that." He saw the security agent wave the next person through the metal detector.

"Good, because I was."

"Think we'll look suspicious?"

"Why?"

"No bags."

It took another minute for the next two people to walk through. Then a rotund man in a gray suit walked through and the security agent held a hand up. The man tilted his head in annoyance as his outline was traced with a metal wand. It beeped when it went over the man's wrist. He pulled his sleeve up to reveal a watch with a wide metal wristband.

"Gray suit's going to make us miss our flight," Mike joked to Ron.

After going through the screening process again, the man was cleared through. "Thanks for nothing, buddy," he remarked.

"Just doing my job, sir. Be safe."

The man mumbled something, but Ron didn't catch it.

One after another, Mike and Ron showed their boarding passes and uneventfully passed through. A few minutes later, they arrived at the waiting area. Judging by the number of people present, the small jet would be completely full.

Ron looked over his boarding pass. "We'll probably board in fifteen minutes or so."

"Good."

Ron looked out the large windows. The sky was becoming a darker shade of blue, and feathery clouds reflected orange and purple hues from the setting sun. He didn't want to think and considered the trip as an opportunity to change his focus. He remembered what the sergeant had told him and shook his head.

"I can see something's on your mind."

"Just thinking of Anne."

Mike pursed his lips together. He didn't say anything.

As Ron sat, he found his eyes becoming heavy. "Maybe I will sleep on the plane." He looked down at Mike's boarding pass and realized the seats weren't next to each other. "You bought both of these tickets at the same time?"

"Yeah."

"The seats are 6B and 15B."

Mike tapped his boarding pass. "We got the last two tickets. I hope the seats are far enough apart for you."

Ron laughed. "I'll live."

"I'm happy to hear you say that."

An hour later, the commuter jet was halfway over Indiana on the way to Chicago. Ron was near the back in seat 15B. The well-dressed person beside him had brought two carry-ons and since the overhead bins were full, one of the small bags was stowed under the seat in front him, which left little leg room. After the plane took off, Ron had extended his legs into the aisle. He faded in and out of a shallow nap. The man in the gray suit was across the aisle.

"Hey, buddy, do you mind?"

Ron's third attempt at slumber failed.

"Buddy. Move your legs already."

Ron realized the man across the aisle was talking to him. In his head, he thought Gray Suit should be called Grouchy Suit. "Oh, sorry. You need to get out?" Ron pulled his legs in front of him.

"No, but the aisle should be clear at all times, buddy."

"So, you don't need to get out?"

"You got a problem, buddy?"

With no expression, Ron looked at the man. He didn't want to provoke him, but that didn't seem to matter. He extended his legs back into the aisle.

Gray Suit cracked his neck as he rolled his head from shoulder to shoulder. "I think you need an attitude adjustment, friend."

Ron leaned toward the guy. "I'm not your friend, your buddy or your verbal punching bag. We'll be in landing in another ten or fifteen minutes, so don't you worry about where I put my legs."

The man recoiled a few inches. He met Ron's gaze and the lines on his shiny forehead grew more defined as his frown deepened. "The emergency exit's right up there," he pointed. "Why don't you go take a flying leap? The world doesn't need ignorant pieces of garbage like you."

The exasperation Ron felt caused his fingers to shake. He held the man's gaze but didn't reply.

"I said, why don't you do the rest of us a favor and just end it," the man whispered in the coldest manner he could muster.

Ron looked away from the man and over the sleeping woman beside him to look out the window. The sky was dark enough so that a handful of stars were shining. It looked very peaceful outside the plane.

"Idiot," he heard the man mumble. He thought of the incident and a hundred different things to say that might be on par with the daggers that leapt off the man's tongue. Instead, he laid back and closed his eyes. The hint of a smile crossed his face.

After the plane landed, Ron felt refreshed. It taxied to the gate, and the passengers went about gathering their carry-on items. Gray Suit stepped into the aisle and reached into the overhead bin. He rudely bumped Ron with his hip.

As the passengers were deplaning, Ron followed Gray Suit toward the exit. "I want to thank you."

Gray Suit glanced behind him? "Oh, you. Yeah, right. For what?"

"For reminding me how to not treat people."

"Whatever, buddy."

"It's no way to go through life."

"Yeah, I care."

Ron thought of what the old man back at the diner said. "I choose to." He felt a wave of calm.

The two of them didn't exchange any more words. When Ron saw a young man with anxious eyes waiting to deplane from two rows up, he stopped to let the guy out.

Ron followed the rest of the passengers down the walkway. When he entered the waiting area, he saw Mike.

"How was your flight?" Mike asked.

"Okay. And you?"

"I was sitting beside the nicest woman. We had a great chat. Would you like to . . ." Mike held a hand up. "Sorry, I think I already know the answer."

Ron wondered why Mike stopped talking then remembered that he had always told Mike he didn't want to hear anything from him for most of the day. He chuckled. "Maybe later."

"I can live with later."

"I need to get the New York boarding pass from you."

"You're assuming I still want you to come."

Ron didn't answer. He saw Gray Suit at the customer service counter. Probably filing a formal complaint about the guy who had his legs in the aisle.

"Okay, bad joke." Mike pulled a pair of boarding passes from his pocket and handed one to Ron.

Ron noted the flight number. "If it's on time, we have less than an hour to get to the gate." He walked toward a set of monitors along the main corridor and scanned until he found their flight. He looked down and ran his hand through his hair. "Unbelievable."

"Why, what is it? You're acting like it's been canceled." Mike scanned the monitors for their flight. "Unbelievable."

"Maybe we can get rerouted. Let's find a customer service agent."

"A CS agent here? In a busy airport?"

Ron ignored Mike's comment and walked away.

"That was supposed to be a joke." Mike followed Ron and caught up with him. He walked beside him as they hiked down the wide corridor. "I'll just follow you. You know the air traffic system better than I do."

"The commercial aspect is a different animal from the small plane I fly."

"Okay."

"But it's not the end of the world if we don't get there tonight, right?"

Mike looked away with a raised eyebrow.

Chapter 14
Rerouted

"What time's Naomi expecting you?" Ron asked.

"About that."

"You told her you were . . ." Ron paused. "You didn't. You never told her you were coming."

"No."

Ron put his hand on Mike's back and directed him toward an empty waiting area. "So *that's* why you wanted me to come along. This woman's already upset and you plan on surprising her? Should we send her a severed head first to make sure she's good and relaxed?"

"No, it's not like that at all."

"Then what is it?"

"Well, it's . . ." Mike looked at the gray carpet. He looked back up at Ron. "Okay, it's like you said."

"That's a rotten thing to do. I'm out."

"I need closure, Ron."

"What are you talking about?"

"For the past two years, how I left things with Naomi bothered me."

"I thought you said you wanted to visit for her benefit, not yours."

"That's right."

"With a surprise visit? You think you'll just walk in, the two of you will have a nice cry and reminisce about how wonderful her sister was and then you'll both happily waltz your separate ways into the future?"

"Of course not. It doesn't work like that."

"Then how does it work? Because I've been wondering that since the day my family died."

Mike's jaw clenched. "I don't know. I don't think anyone knows. Sometimes, a man just knows when there's something incomplete in his life, so he does what he needs to do to make it right."

"Some things can't be made right."

"Okay, not right, but not as wrong as before."

Ron mulled the statement over. "You can't change the past."

"You're right. But you can change your reaction to it."

"My reaction is irrelevant." Ron waited for an argument, but didn't get one.

"I'm sorry for dragging you into this."

They both stood there for another minute. "We've come this far. Let's go see what customer service has to say," Ron said.

Ron saw the counter for customer service was open with no line. There were two women behind the counter. When one of them saw the two men approaching, she disappeared through a door behind the counter. The other woman looked tired.

"Kill 'em with kindness," Ron whispered.

The lone woman in a dark blue jacket over a white collared blouse greeted them. "How are you two gentlemen doing this evening?"

"Great, and you?" Ron said.

The woman perked up as if no one had been cordial with her all day. "If I were any better, there would have to be two of me."

"That sounds like someone who's getting off work soon," Ron smiled.

"You got it." She smiled back. "So what can I do to make your evening even better?"

"We'll be doing much better once we get rerouted to New York. We just got off our first flight and saw that the connecting flight was canceled."

"I'm sorry to hear that. Let me see your boarding passes and I'll see what I can do."

The two men handed her their passes, and she started typing while fixating on the screen. "I don't see any problems. Your flight to New York leaves on time from gate H9. You only have about twenty minutes before it starts boarding."

"Are you sure?" Ron said. "When we checked the monitors a few minutes ago, they indicated the flight was canceled."

"Hmm. Oh, I see what happened. There was a maintenance issue that made them cancel it, but apparently it's resolved." She handed the boarding passes back. "Is there anything else?"

"What sort of maintenance issue?" Mike asked. Ron heard the anxiety in Mike's voice.

She shook her head. "It doesn't say."

"As long as it's resolved," Ron said. He, too, wanted to know what was going on with the plane but knew there was little chance any useful information was available for the woman to share. "Okay, thanks."

The two men walked down the main corridor toward the departure gate. "What do you think is going on with the plane?" Mike asked.

"Don't know. But if it's resolved, then that's all that matters."

A young woman who held the hand of a girl walked toward them. Her other hand towed a black carry-on bag with a doll resting on top of it. Twice, Ron saw the girl look behind her, and he assumed she was checking to make sure the doll was still there. He wondered why she wasn't holding it. As the two pairs passed, the girl looked up at Ron and smiled.

"Hi," she said.

He smiled back at her.

Her mom yanked her hand to bring her closer. "We don't talk to strangers, Lucy, remember?"

"He looked like he needed someone to be nice to him."

"Don't be nice to people. They'll always want something more from you."

"He didn't want anything from me. Didn't you see his face?"

Ron heard the woman talking in a low tone to the girl as the distance between them increased, but he couldn't hear anything else.

"She seemed like a sweet kid," Mike said.

"Yeah." Ron felt his strength drain at the reminder that he had lost his own child. He wanted to duck into one of the darkened waiting areas where he could hide and curl up in the fetal position on the chairs. Every couple, child and family he saw was salt poured into the wound of what he had lost, and he was tired of the endless reminders. He blinked slowly as they walked, and read random advertisements on the wall or in passing shops to distract his mind from the vortex that kept spinning and agitating his pain.

When the two men arrived at gate H9 ten minutes later, the plane was already boarding.

Sweat clung to Ron's forehead. He was busy battling his own thoughts. "It looks like the plane's doing fine."

Mike looked at Ron. "It's not the plane I'm worried about now. Are you okay?"

"Don't worry about me. You never need to worry about me."

Mike patted him on the back. "Not that it matters, but you can worry about me."

Ron remembered what Mike had told him about his situation. It changed Ron's focus, but only until he passed a man on the plane talking to a boy seated next to him.

Once again, Mike and Ron were rows apart. This time, Ron had a window seat near the back of the plane. An elderly woman took the aisle seat in the same row.

Shortly after the jet departed, Ron dozed off.

"Honey, wake up."

Ron felt a gentle kiss on his cheek. A couple seconds later, he felt a soft kiss on his lips. He opened his eyes and saw Anne lying next to him. The bedroom was bright with the morning sun, which Ron found perfectly accented with her smile.

She ran a hand through his hair and traced his sideburns. He felt her palm against his face as she leaned in and kissed him again.

He felt his heartbeat rapidly increase. He suddenly grabbed her wrists.

Her eyes widened. "What are you doing?"

"Don't go," he pleaded.

"But I have to." She struggled to break free. "You already know that."

"You don't need to do this."

He felt the fight die out of her. She slowly shook her head. "It's already happened."

"Please. Don't leave me."

"It's not my choice."

"Then it's mine." The room dimmed.

She blinked as tears streamed from her eyes. "No, it's not."

"What can I do?"

"Let go."

"I can't."

"Then I'll only haunt you," she cried. "Is that what you want?"

Ron felt his own tears break. "No."

"Then let me go. This is cruel."

"Don't do this to me," he pleaded. "God knows how much I love you." He slowly released his grip on her wrists.

With her fingertips, she gently wiped fresh tears off his cheek. "I'm not doing this to you. *You're* doing this to you." She shook her head. "Don't remember me like this. Don't remember us like this. You need to let go."

"I'm not that strong. Can't you see that?"

"Be strong enough to let go."

Ron's eyes searched his wife's for answers. She blinked, which caused more tears to trace her already tear-stained cheeks. As she pulled her hands away, he saw that her wrists were black with bruises from where he had held so tight. He saw the pain on her face, and he hated himself for it.

Ron felt a tap on his shoulder. He opened his eyes, and the woman beside him pointed toward the flight stewardess. He wondered why the woman didn't just let him sleep, but when part of his dream flashed in his head, he was glad he had been pulled out of it.

"Would you like a drink, sir?"

After a few seconds, he realized where he was. He shifted in his seat. "A ginger ale would be good."

The stewardess poured his drink and handed the cup to him.

"Thanks."

Ron sipped the drink and looked out the window. He overheard the woman next to him request the same drink. He glanced at his watch and figured the plane was over Pennsylvania. Clusters of glowing lights from small towns interrupted the blackness below.

"It's been a long day, hasn't it," the woman beside him said in a matter-of-fact manner.

"Pardon?"

She pointed toward the plastic cup on his tray. "You and I got the same drink. I was guessing that you had a stressful day."

"You have no idea."

"I hope tomorrow goes better."

Tomorrow. For the first time, Ron thought of the next day. He hadn't planned on being around for it, but with his commitment to remain by his new friend's side, he now had a reason to be there. Surreptitiously, he could see the woman was still looking his way. Apparently, she wanted to talk but he didn't.

"Me too," he finally replied.

"Are you flying to New York to see family?"

Ron saw Mike dodging elbows jutting into the aisle as he walked toward where Ron and the woman were seated.

Mike stopped and placed a hand on top of the seat in front of the woman. He leaned over. "I'm up in seat 9C. Would you mind switching seats with me so I can sit by my friend?"

"Oh, well I suppose that'd be alright."

Ron noticed she acted somewhat flustered.

"I'll hold your drink if that would help."

"Yes, yes it would." She handed her drink to Ron. "I just need to grab my purse. It's under the seat." She put her tray table up and grabbed her purse. She stood up but remained slightly crouched to avoid hitting the overhead bin and stepped out into the aisle.

Ron offered her drink back to her. She took it, whispered something to Mike, and left.

Mike sat down in the seat and fastened the seat belt. "The seat's pre-warmed. That's a nice service, isn't it?"

Ron shook his head. "What did she whisper to you?"

"Something about the guy next to her not being much for conversation, as if he were dead or something like that."

"She may have been right."

"She's in a better place now and so am I."

Ron looked out the window. The plane passed through a beacon-lit cloud that was flashing red. Ron found the pattern both hypnotizing and relaxing. It allowed him to focus on nothing in particular.

After a couple minutes passed, Mike spoke again. "I was hoping we could talk more before we get to New York."

"Let me guess . . . Naomi?" Ron said as he continued to stare out the window. "You haven't told me much about her, but you've told me enough."

"What do you think?"

"Like you said, she'll still be angry with you." He figured she'd be even less happy with Mike when he showed up unannounced at her doorstep in an hour, assuming that was the plan. He considered saying as much, but decided not to since Mike already looked anxious enough.

"I know."

Ron looked at Mike. "I can't say I blame her. If your brother had some sort of obsession with your wife, how could you miss that?"

Mike frowned as he clenched his hands together. "Everyone says hindsight is twenty-twenty. But even in hindsight, I can't say I saw it coming. Maybe we just want to think highly of those we love."

Ron thought of Anne. She was flawless. He couldn't recall a single thing she had done wrong. Had they ever fought? It had to have been his fault if they had. Even her driving had been perfect - other than the scrape on the front bumper from when a light pole in a parking lot had jumped in front of the car. It couldn't have been her fault. If it weren't for the truck driver who was clearly getting away with murder, he'd be home with her and his son right now. He closed his eyes in the realization that he wasn't remembering her clearly.

"You're right," Ron said. "I'm not so sure hindsight is twenty-twenty when it comes to family. We see them through lenses that hide their flaws."

Mike nodded. "Perhaps that's what I'm doing."

"What else do I need to know about Naomi?"

Mike took a deep breath and exhaled. "She was the older sister. Actually, she was Helen's adopted older sister. Helen's parents didn't think they were ever going to be able to have kids, so they took the adoption route and found Naomi. Two years later, her mom finally got pregnant and had Helen.

"When Helen came along, Naomi was three. From what Helen told me, they really neglected Naomi for a while since they finally had a child of their own. They always loved both girls, but I think Naomi felt like a guest who had worn out her welcome. In spite of that, she and Helen grew up as best friends. I'd have to admit that Naomi had more street smarts than Helen. She was just really savvy when it came to matters involving people. She was generally a strong judge of character. But at the same time, she can be emotional, and she flies off the handle pretty fast when provoked."

"When someone kills your sister, that's quite a provocation. Can't say I blame her."

"She was my wife, Ron."

"I know. And I'm sorry." Ron could see Mike was shaken.

"Anyway, I know she still blames me for it."

"What does she do? I mean what kind of work?"

Mike laughed. "Would you believe she has a Pilates studio?"

"Today, I would believe just about anything. Married?"

"Just to her cat if she still has it."

"Have you spoken to her since you lost Helen?"

"Only to her mom. From what she tells me, Naomi's as angry with me now as she was two years ago. She's bi-polar and prone to mood swings, which can be sudden."

"I don't understand what you think you're going to say in person that couldn't be said over the phone."

Mike looked at Ron. "You're right. But it isn't about what's said. It's about taking the time to be there. It's the only way I know how to show her I care and that I'm sorry."

Ron rubbed his chin. He tried to empathize with Mike but was having a difficult time of it. He took a sip of ginger ale. It occurred to him that when he was thinking of what Mike was dealing with, he wasn't thinking about what he himself was going through. He told himself the distraction was healthy. It might even help to save his life.

"I hope she'll see me."

"She will."

"What makes you so sure?"

"Because the two of us make for a strong team." Ron wasn't sure exactly why he said that. But the emotion he saw in Mike's eyes told him that it was the right thing to say.

"Thank you," Mike whispered.

Ron finished his ginger ale and tried to relax as he considered what Mike had told him about Helen and Naomi. The seatbelt sign lit up, and the captain announced there was turbulence ahead.

Chapter 15

Wheel of Life

Ron didn't find the turbulence nerve-wracking, but he noticed Mike's grip on the armrest.

"You okay, Mike?"

"Sure," Mike nodded.

The plane hit another bump, and Ron watched the heads of passengers in front of him move in unison as if choreographed by an unseen power.

The captain announced for the flight attendants to prepare the cabin for landing.

Ron leaned toward Mike. "They always say they can't land the plane unless everyone is buckled in and the seats are upright, but I can assure you, once the plane's out of fuel, it's going to land one way or the other." He noticed Mike loosened his grip on the armrest as he laughed.

"I think that's the first time you've joked all day."

"The turbulence shook it out of me."

"That's two."

Ron smiled. He'd rather be flying his own plane, but

sometimes it was relaxing to let the airlines do the work. And if they were getting jolted this much in a plane this size, the bounces in a smaller plane would be rougher.

A flight attendant passed, collected Ron's cup and reminded him to put his tray table up. Fifteen minutes later, the wheels chirped onto the well-lit runway at LaGuardia.

Mike looked at his watch. "Just after nine."

"So now what? We visit with Naomi then take the red-eye back?"

"I don't think she'd appreciate late night visitors - especially me. I've already made reservations for a hotel. You'll get your own room."

"You weren't kidding about all expenses paid." Ron again peered through the window. He watched a jet take off as their plane taxied toward the terminal. He wondered if Mike was going into debt to pay for the trip. New York was expensive. He thought of asking, but upon running a few numbers in his head, he figured Mike wasn't spending any more than someone would spend on a vacation. Still, he found the situation unusual. But the whole day had been unusual.

The plane stopped, and the seatbelt sign dimmed with the familiar tone.

Twenty minutes later, Ron followed Mike into a cab.

"No bags?" the cabby asked.

"No bags," Mike echoed. "Waldorf Astoria, please."

"You got it," the cabby replied.

Ron's eyes widened. "We're staying at the Waldorf Astoria? Isn't that a little pricey?"

"I told you already. I got it."

Ron felt uncomfortable. He wasn't used to having someone pay his way.

The cab raced onto the expressway and dodged vehicles like they were on an amusement park ride.

"We'll need to stop somewhere for clothes and provisions," Ron said.

"Already done."

"You had this all planned out?"

"I planned it from Toledo." Mike looked at Ron. "I used to work in the city. Don't worry. I've already made the arrangements for what we need."

"I see." Ron's curiosity finally got the best of him. "I never did find out what you did."

"I thought you'd never ask." Mike laughed. "When Helen and I lived here, I was a data analyst."

"I'm not sure what that is."

"Don't feel bad. Not many people understood what I did back then, even when I explained it."

"You changed jobs?"

"After Helen passed, I left. I wanted something with less stress."

"That's when you started hitch-hiking on small planes?"

Mike laughed. "Not exactly. There was some time in between that. I guess you could say I was doing some soul searching. Meaning of life kind of stuff."

"What did you find?"

Through passing lights, Ron saw the smile fade from Mike's face.

"I'm still searching." Mike paused. "And while you work to resolve one problem, something worse always comes up."

Ron slowly nodded in partial understanding. He wanted to tell Mike he agreed, but didn't want to admit he felt the same. He watched the heavy traffic keeping pace with the cab. "What does a data analyst do in New York?"

"At the time, I worked for a hedge fund."

"Sounds stressful." Ron knew enough about the stock market to know that hedge funds figured out ways to make money no matter what the market did. At least the ones that stayed in business did. He wondered how Mike had done.

"It paid well. What else would you like to know?"

Ron found himself bombarded with a plethora of questions about Mike's past, but what he really wanted to know was how to make the pain go away when you lose your family. He already knew Mike didn't have the answer to that. He wanted to change the subject. "How much longer to the hotel?" He asked while staring out the window and watching lights reflect off the wet pavement. "It's been a long day."

"From here, not much longer. But one traffic accident will make a liar out of me."

The cab merged onto 495 and went through the Queens Midtown Tunnel. Even without getting out of the cab, Ron felt that being immersed in New York City was an experience that couldn't be captured in pictures. He'd traveled to Los Angeles on business, but the feel was different on the west coast. No palm trees here. After a few turns on the busy streets, the cab stopped in front of the hotel.

"Waldorf Astoria," the cabby announced with an inflection that could announce royalty.

Ron opened the door and got out. Mike paid the cabby opening the driver's door while saying, "Let me get your bags."

"We didn't bring any," Mike said.

"Oh, that's right," the cabby said as he pulled the door shut. "Who travels without bags?"

"People who'd rather not have baggage." Mike scooted across the seat and exited the same door as Ron.

Ron was looking up the front of building. "I guess this will do."

Mike laughed. "Follow me."

They entered the lobby and walked up the steps. "Look around," Mike said. "The place will certainly take your mind off things, won't it?"

Ron was about to agree when he saw a man spin a young girl in a yellow dress as if they were ballroom dancing. They were probably influenced by the piano music. A woman who Ron presumed to be the girl's mother was talking to another couple when she heard her daughter's laughter and looked over with a smile.

"It almost does," Ron said as he again glanced in the direction of the family.

"Take a look at that clock." Mike pointed to a nine foot tall bronze clock with a base of marble and stained wood. "Wouldn't that look great in your living room?"

"I'd need a bigger house."

They walked past the young family and the girl waved at Ron. She reminded him of the girl at the airport.

"I'm going to check in and get the room keys. I'll check with the concierge to make sure everything is prepared in the rooms." Mike tilted his head toward the area they just walked through. "Take a look around. You'll be surprised how much you already missed."

"Good idea."

Ron walked back toward the area where they had entered. The grand chandelier held his attention until he neared a set of steps, which descended toward a large mosaic. He stood by one of the large Pompeian square columns and stared at the mosaic, which was fourteen feet in diameter. Ron wondered how he could've missed it on the way in, but the scale of the place was much to absorb.

"Beautiful, isn't it?" An old man's voice interrupted Ron's concentration. Beside him stood a short elderly man in a dark blue suit with a red tie. He leaned on a cane of ebony wood. Ron guessed the man's age to be upper eighties.

"It is."

"They call it the Wheel of Life." The old man pointed toward the mosaic. "I'm that picture there. It's toward the end of the circle," he laughed.

Ron stared at the mosaic as the old man spoke. He assumed the man was talking about the scene that depicted the end of one's life.

"The end of the circle," Leonard repeated. "Do circles have an end?" He waved his hand as if brushing away a bothersome fly. "Ah, no matter. I'm not afraid. Nope, old Leonard here isn't afraid of anything."

The old man's confidence made Ron wonder if he had any idea what it was like to lose what Ron had lost.

"Which one are you?" Leonard looked at Ron's hand and tapped the wedding ring on it. He pointed toward the mosaic again with his cane. "Ah, I bet the family right there is you, isn't it? Here with your family, are you?"

Ron winced at the old man's words. He knew the man meant no harm, but it still stung. He studied the mosaic and shook his head. "I'm not on there."

"Are you sure? Why, a young fellow such as yourself with a family is right there." Leonard pointed toward the part of the mosaic that depicted a couple with a baby.

"My family's dead," Ron blurted out. "Killed in a car crash."

Chapter 16

Leonard

Ron caught the old man who nearly buckled. Leonard leaned on his cane as Ron kept him upright.

"I had no idea," he said.

"Let's have a seat over here." Ron escorted Leonard to a chair in an area that overlooked the mosaic.

"I'm so sorry. I didn't know."

"I know. Don't worry about it."

"I didn't know," Leonard said again as he collapsed into the chair.

Ron looked the old man over and saw he was probably fine. "I should—"

With his cane, Leonard rapped the leg of the chair next to him. "Have a seat."

Ron noticed that the man had quickly regained his composure.

"I said sit."

"Why?"

"Because when I look at what you lost, I see myself from fifty years ago."

"I wouldn't wish that on anyone."

"It was recent, was it?"

Ron sat in the chair next to Leonard. He nodded.

"When I was your age," Leonard said slowly, "I went through that."

Ron studied the old man's eyes. They were moist with sincerity.

"You lost your kids too?" Leonard asked.

"My son. We had recently celebrated his first birthday."

Leonard shook his head. "I had two boys. Gone instantly with my beloved Mildred in that car crash."

Ron thought of his situation. "I'm sorry. What happed to the other driver?"

"Other driver? There was no other driver." Leonard gripped his cane tight and banged the foot of it against the floor. "*I* was the driver."

Ron drew back. "I'm sorry."

"I was too for the longest time. I kept blaming myself even though the wheel broke when the car hit a bad hole in the road that night. I know now that there was nothing I could have done."

Ron shook his head. "I'd give anything to go back and change things. Some days I wish I'd never met my wife, then I wouldn't hurt like this."

"Well, now, that's no way to live."

"*This* is living?" Ron's eyes widened.

"You and I both took a risk when we fell in love, young fellow."

"She loved me back. I don't see the risk in that. It was quite safe, really."

"Oh, you want to keep your heart safe?" Leonard leaned toward Ron and squinted at him. "Then never give it to anyone. When you fall in love with someone, you can bet your heart will be run through the ringer. It'll be crushed and hit like there's a war on it. If you want to keep it safe, you can't ever give it to anyone. You hear me? Never give it to anyone."

Ron pondered the old man's words. He tried to think of a rebuttal. After a minute he gave up. "What did you do?"

"I fell in love again. I met Inga." He nodded slowly and smiled. "We fell in love. We got married. We had children together."

Faint piano music continued to fill the air as if to echo the joy the old man had found a second time.

"She passed away last year," Leonard whispered. "But it's okay." He pointed toward the mosaic with his cane. "Circle of life. Someday I'll come full circle and so will you. But before you do, I hope you find someone to travel with. You still have many years ahead of you."

Ron rubbed his head. While most people were encouraged by the notion of having many years ahead of them, he wasn't one of them. Time wasn't what he wanted—control over the chaos was.

Leonard slowly got up and waved Ron away when he rose to help. "I'll be fine. So will you. Deal with today as best you can. Each tomorrow gets better. Take it from old Lenny."

Ron looked up at the old man. "Can I give you hand?"

Leonard waved him off again. "I've gotten myself this far. But I appreciate the kind offer. You have a good evening, young man."

A smile teased its way onto Ron's face as he watched the old man descend the stairs. He reminded Ron of his grandfather, especially the positive attitude.

As people from the past found their way into his present thoughts, Ron found himself lost in the reflection of crystals from the chandelier. Like suspended tears from heaven, they remained in place as he patiently waited for them to fall and shatter on the mosaic below and conclude the circle of life.

"There you are."

Ron recognized Mike's voice. He turned and saw him approaching with two small envelopes in hand.

"Isn't this place gorgeous?"

"Incredible," Ron said as he ignored the atmosphere and thought more of his impromptu conversation with Leonard.

Mike extended a hand with an envelope. "Here's your room key. Everything should be in order. I had to guess your size, so I hope the clothes fit. I worked at a tailor's briefly during my first semester of college — just thought I'd throw that in. If they don't fit, call the concierge and he'll deliver anything you need."

Ron rose from the chair. "A new wardrobe?"

"This trip has some nice perks. You can eat at one of the restaurants or order room service. Charge it to the room. Remember, I got it."

"You might regret that."

Mike put a hand on Ron's shoulder. "No. No, I won't."

Ron nodded. "What time do we head out tomorrow?"

"If I've done my homework correctly, we should try to meet Naomi at her place around 9:30. She rarely leaves before then on her days off."

"How do you know that?"

"Like I said earlier, I analyze data. That includes knowing where to find what you need to know."

"Very resourceful." Ron wanted to suggest they were planning an ambush, but at the moment he was craving sleep more than anything else.

Mike looked toward the stairs where two middle-aged women dressed to the nines were carefully descending in high heels. "I think you already have some idea of that after today."

Ron chuckled. "Isn't that the truth. What time should I meet you back here? Nine?"

"Let's make it a quarter 'til."

"See you then." Ron slapped Mike on the shoulder and walked toward the elevators.

Chapter 17

Day Two

Ron slid the key through the slot and opened the door to the room. He turned the light on and paused for a moment to soak in the opulence. Wide stripes of white and cream on the walls began at the crown molding and terminated at waist level into white wainscoting. Columns similar to the Pompeian ones in the lobby were tastefully integrated into the walls. Ron thought the furnishings could all have come out of a European palace. "I wish I could share this with Anne," he whispered as he closed the door.

On the bed, he saw pajamas and the complete set of clothes that he'd wear the next day. The pants were casual beige and the blue pullover shirt complimented them. Ron wondered how Mike knew he preferred pullover shirts to button-up, but he chalked that up to coincidence. Next to the blue shirt was a buttoned dress shirt with a striped tie tucked in by the collar. A note atop the shirt stated, *I'll be wearing one like this. You choose. Tie optional.* A charcoal sport jacket completed the outfit. He slipped his shoes off and set them by the closet.

He was a little hungry, so he flipped though the hotel guide on the desk until he found the room service menu and ordered a grilled chicken sandwich, vegetable medley and iced tea. He arranged for it to be delivered in twenty minutes, which gave him time for a shower. By habit, he went to charge his phone, but he didn't have a charger with him. He called the concierge who said the hotel had a charger for his model phone he could use. Ron asked him to send it up with room service.

The soothing shower left Ron alone with his thoughts. As the water ran over his face, he closed his eyes and images of the day and the people he'd met drifted by. It occurred to him that he should call Jerry's wife and apologize for his conduct. She didn't deserve his rudeness. Maybe he'd send their family a postcard. No, a phone call would be more appropriate. Plus, he didn't know their address.

He wondered if Carly had spoken with Jerry.

But of everyone he'd met that day, Bradley had left the deepest impression on him. The boy reminded him so much of what he expected from a son. The thought of offering to adopt Bradley exited his head as quickly as it had entered. It was an absurd idea. But perhaps he could fly over to the airport from time to time to take Bradley flying. Then again, it'd be better for the kid to have flying lessons when he was older. Still, he felt a connection with the kid and wanted him to know he cared.

He shook his head. He felt ridiculous for feeling an attachment to a kid he'd just met. It was probably due to his temporary mental state that day, or maybe he was just trying to fill the void left from the loss of his own son.

He'd just finished showering when he heard a knock on the door. He donned a robe and opened the door to receive the meal he'd requested. The phone charger was on the tray. He plugged it into the wall, then connected his phone. Afterwards, he enjoyed his meal. A half-hour later, he was asleep.

Ron put his forearm over his eyes to protect them from the light. He was sure he'd feel his wife's touch any second since he often met her when he dreamed.

After a few moments, his arm slumped to his side as his eyes opened. He looked around and saw he was in the same hotel room where he had fallen asleep the night before. Not a dream.

He rolled onto his side and saw the clock. 7:33.

He couldn't recall what he had dreamt. How did it go with Anne? He wished he could remember whether she had appeared in one of his dreams, even if it was unpleasant. At least he would've seen her. He was troubled by how he remembered her, and sometimes he felt like an addict who needed a fix.

After rising and placing a call to room service for breakfast, Ron took a quick shower and dressed. After he ate, he enjoyed another cup of coffee while savoring the view of the city from the window. He downed the last of the java and set the cup on the tray.

As he crossed the room, he caught a glimpse of himself in the mirror. It reminded him of the mirror back home, the one shattered by the misfiring gun that refused to kill him. He couldn't believe that was only twenty-four hours ago. He took a few steps back to study his reflection. The image was no longer as shattered as the one back home. It wasn't as polished as it was before the accident, but not quite as troubled as yesterday's likeness either.

Ron didn't know if he'd be returning to the room. He hung his old clothes in the closet, tucked the room key into his wallet and pulled the door shut when left. It locked with a loud click that reminded him of the clicks from the previous morning. Today would be different. He had inadvertently made a new friend in record time, a friend who calmed the current tempest in life by opening his eyes to the plights of others in a manner different than what he was accustomed to. It felt ironic since counseling was his career. He never expected to be the one receiving.

No, he wasn't receiving counseling. But the more he thought of the situation, the more confusing it was. It wasn't formal help, but it had a similar impact — no, a stronger impact. It wasn't theory; it was practical work out in the field.

The situation made him wonder how well he had truly connected with his patients or helped them. Now, he wasn't just seeing the problems so many people lived with, he was experiencing them, too.

Ron exited the elevator and found Mike sitting in a chair near one of the large Pompeian columns.

Mike was dressed as if attending an important business meeting. When he looked up from the paper, he saw Ron approaching. "Good morning. It's beautiful out there today."

"Morning. The view from the room was impressive. A guy could get used to this."

"You should see the view from higher up."

The phrase *higher up* made Ron think of Anne. He winced at the thought, but the hurt was less from the additional layer of time that had accumulated since yesterday.

"I hope you're ready for Pilates with Naomi. She should have room for a couple stragglers, wouldn't you agree?"

"I don't think we're quite dressed for that." Ron saw a trio of men in pinstriped suits descending the stairs. Each one had a briefcase in hand. "This may be more like a court hearing."

Mike sighed. "I've been thinking about that all night." He folded the paper and set it on the small table next to the chair. He appeared troubled. "How would you feel about turning around and flying back to Toledo?"

"Sure, let's go."

"I was hoping for an argument."

Ron chuckled. "I know. That's why you brought me, to help you see this through. And that's what I'm going to do, so let's go see Naomi."

Mike rubbed his chin while his eyes searched the room distractedly.

"Where do you plan on meeting her?" Ron asked

"I figured it'd be best to meet at her apartment."

Ron nodded as he remembered what Mike had said that last evening. "Are you going to call first?"

"Then she'd be sure to be out by the time we got there."

"You don't know that."

"You don't know how much she hates me."

Ron cringed at the thought of surprising the woman. "You might get maced."

"Or tased."

Ron smiled. "Let's get a cab and find out which."

Mike laughed. He rose and they descended the stairs to Park Avenue where the doorman hailed a cab. Mike handed the cabby a note with the address. "Here, please."

The cabby looked at the address. "You got it," he said in an accent that Ron couldn't place. Maybe Russian. The cab launched into traffic.

"Have you thought of what you're going to say to her?" Ron asked.

"It kept me from sleeping. I've thought of a thousand different things to say. But how do you tell someone something they already know?"

"What do you mean?"

"She already knows the details behind everything that happened, and she blames me for Helen's death. I've accepted that, and I don't blame her for it. But even so, she still holds so much anger inside." Mike looked out the window and shook his head. "Living with that anger is affecting her life."

Ron thought about the anger he felt toward the truck driver who killed his family. The premonition reminded him that he still needed to review the police report. At a minimum he wanted to confront the truck driver in court. Justice would be done even if Ron had to administer it himself. He felt tension build within and found it easy to empathize with Naomi. He tried to put aside his need for instant justice, and decided it best to be supportive of Mike right now. "How do you plan on helping her?"

"I want her to let it go. I'll do anything to make that happen." Mike took a deep breath and exhaled. "I'm ready for it."

"You make it sound like she might kill you," Ron whispered.

Mike's gaze lowered. "Whatever it takes."

Ron recognized the look on Mike's face. It was a countenance Ron had shared the day prior. He understood why Mike couldn't do this alone. "I'll be right there with you. No matter what, we're going to get through this."

Mike looked at Ron through moist eyes and smiled.

The cab stopped on a tree-lined street with townhouses. "Here we are," the cabby announced.

"Ready to do this?" Ron said.

Mike slowly nodded, but said, "No."

"Come on," Ron said as he exited the cab.

Mike paid the cabby and followed.

There were sets of steps in front of each townhome entryway every car-length or two. The faces of the buildings were either brick or stone. Some were painted. Mike pointed toward a set of stairs in front of a gray brick building that was between red brick and beige stone buildings. "Up these steps."

The two men walked side by side up the wide steps. Mike rang the bell to Naomi's apartment. After a few seconds, a man toting a bike opened the door. Ron guessed the guy to be in his late twenties. He wore faded jeans and a black t-shirt with a metal band's logo on it. "If you guys are looking for the place for rent it was taken yesterday, sorry," he said as he pushed passed them. Mike stuck his foot in the doorway just enough so the door didn't latched shut.

"Was it Naomi's old place?" Mike asked. He saw her name by the buzzer he'd pressed.

"No, man. Grumpy Girl's still here," the man said as he carried his bike down the steps.

Ron laughed.

"Grumpy Girl?" Mike echoed.

The man mounted his bike. "Yeah, man. I don't know what her problem is. Sometimes she walks around wearing these tight little yoga pants as if she wants attention, if you know what I mean, but every guy I know who's tried to talk to her says she just blows him off."

"So she blew you off," Ron said.

The man rolled his eyes. "Like either of you have a shot. Good luck." He pedaled down the street.

"Maybe she's not home," Ron said.

"She is."

"What makes you so sure?"

"Just . . ." Mike paused. "I know she is. Let's go." He opened the door and entered. Ron followed him in and they went up one flight of stairs. Mike knocked on the door. They heard footsteps from the behind the door. Ron saw the peephole darken for a second.

"I'm not home," said a female voice from the other side of the door.

"Naomi, it's me."

"I know who it is," Naomi shouted. "You should be in jail for murder!"

Chapter 18

Something in Common

"We need to talk," Mike said.

The door flew open and Ron saw an angry young woman who could pass for Anne's older sister. The only differences were Naomi's short hair and darker skin tone.

And her attitude.

But even in her upset condition, Ron could see why the young man with the bike hinted at so many guys being attracted to her. She had all the attributes of a magazine cover girl. He could have sworn there was a family resemblance between her and Anne. It was everything he could do to hide the surprise on his face. His face flushed as waves of emotion washed through him, but no one noticed.

Naomi wore black yoga pants and a pink, form-fitting long sleeve pullover. She had a black rain jacket slung over her shoulder. At first, Ron assumed she was about to leave, but he could hear the TV in the background.

"Talk?" She said. "The last thing we ever need to do is *talk*. You know what you need to do?"

"What?"

"Leave." She stepped forward and pushed him. The hallway wall stopped him from tumbling backward. "Get out of here."

He regained his composure and stood up straight. "Not until we talk."

"Fine. I'll make you a deal." She put her free hand on her hip.

"What is it?"

"Swim over to Jersey and back, and we'll talk."

Expressionless, Mike looked at Ron then back at Naomi.

Naomi looked at Ron. "You know he can't even swim?" She looked Mike up and down. "This one. Pathetic." She looked back at Ron. "Who are you?" Her demeanor remained sour.

"Ron. Ron McQuillen." He extended his hand, which she ignored. He let it drop.

"He ever tell you everyone around him dies? They all end up dead!" She screamed. "Now leave, you're making me late for work."

"You have today off," Mike said.

Ron turned toward the noise of someone opening a door. It closed just as quickly. The tension between Mike and Naomi was making him sweat as he felt a panic attack trying to overwhelm him.

"How'd you know that? Still doing that stalking crap? No one's sued you yet?" She looked at Ron. "That's all he does. It's his business. Some kind of stalking."

"It's data analysis," Mike said.

"People aren't data!" Naomi screamed. "But now my sister is, isn't she? She's another statistical piece of data thanks to your crazy brother!" She turned to Ron and said, "Why on earth would I ever listen to you!"

"Because my wife's dead!" Ron yelled. He regretted saying it before the last word rolled off his lips, but he needed the tension release. Saying it out loud forced him to acknowledge something he hated.

"What happened? He killed her, too?" She screamed while staring Mike in the eyes.

Mike shuddered as Ron shook his head.

"No," Ron said in a calm voice as tears quickly revealed his emotional state. "I . . ." He tilted his head toward Mike. "We're just here because we both know the pain." He slapped his chest a few times with his palm. "*I* know the pain you're living with."

Ron waited for Mike to say something, but Mike remained reticent. He saw the tears forming in Naomi's eyes as she searched his for sincerity.

"Naomi," Ron said in practically a whisper. "You and I and Mike all suffered the worst kind of loss. It's the worst thing to have in common."

Naomi crossed her arms and looked up, then down a few seconds later.

"I don't want to live like this, holding this kind of pain and resentment forever. Do you?"

"Then don't," Naomi said through pursed lips. "Just end it."

Ron saw her fingers digging into her upper arms as she clung tightly to herself.

"I tried to," Ron said.

"What?" Naomi asked, drawing in a breath.

Ron tried to speak again but couldn't force the words out. He held up a finger and the only sounds came from the Pilates video playing on the TV in the apartment.

"Yesterday morning," Ron said. He looked away from her. "I tried to commit suicide. I would've gone through with it if Mike hadn't shown up when he had."

For the next minute, neither of them spoke.

"What happened?" Mike whispered.

"At the house, before we met at the airport, I put a gun to my head. It was the weirdest thing. I pulled the trigger a couple times and it wouldn't fire. But then I pointed it at the floor and it did."

"What?" Mike said. Ron could tell he was shocked. "It fired?"

"Yeah."

"How many guns do you have?"

To Ron, that was the oddest possible question. "What difference does that make? You only need one to kill yourself and, not that it's any of your business, but that's the only one I have."

"What kind is it?"

"What kind?" Ron stopped short. "Who cares? What a weird question."

Ron saw Mike's focus drift to the floor. He couldn't make sense of what Mike was trying to ask but suspected Mike knew something he wasn't sharing. Naomi diverted his attention.

Tears had welled in Naomi's eyes. Seconds later, they fell. She bit her lip as she stared at Ron. She turned around and walked back into the apartment.

"Are you okay?" Mike whispered to Ron.

Ron nodded quickly. He was glad Mike could still ask a normal question. They both followed Naomi, who had collapsed onto a brown leather couch. She tossed her coat over the armrest, looked up at Ron and slowly pulled back one of her sleeves. Ron saw the scar on her wrist.

Mike saw it, too. He started shaking his head. "Oh, no, not you, Naomi."

"I couldn't go on," she said. "Helen was all I had. My whole life, she was the only one I ever had. When you got married and took her from me, I was okay with that because I was happy that she was happy. But when . . ."

"I had no idea that . . ." He kept shaking his head. "Everyone around me dies," he whispered.

Ron saw the defeated look on Mike's face. It was a look he'd seen at Anne's funeral from those who were closest to her. He knew the feeling, but he wished he didn't. The other thing that occurred to him was that Mike wasn't always a step ahead in all situations. Apparently the man wasn't as good at predicting the future as he had appeared to be.

Ron's eyes met Naomi's and she smiled weakly at him. She shifted on the couch and motioned for him to sit beside her. He did and remembered Mike said she was bi-polar. He wondered if that was influencing her sudden mood change.

"When did it happen?" she whispered.

"Just over a month ago."

"Oh." She placed a hand over his hand.

"I need to go," Mike said suddenly. He rushed out, and pulled the door behind him. It slammed shut.

Ron tried to get up but Naomi pulled him back down onto the couch. He looked into her moist eyes and saw his own pain reflected back.

"We should go after him," Ron said.

Naomi slowly shook her head. "Stay." She scooted closer so that their legs were pressed together.

Ron was dumbfounded by how quickly her attitude had changed. More than that, she was coming on to him after meeting him just a few minutes ago. When she leaned in to kiss him, Ron leaned away. "What are doing?"

"Don't you feel it?" She asked.

"Feel what?"

"The connection we share."

"What, Mike?"

Naomi slid back a few inches. "Now *that* ruins the mood."

"Naomi, what are you talking about?"

She stared at him for a while and searched his face. "The only credit Schwartz gets is for bringing us together."

Ron realized he didn't know Mike's last name until just now. It wasn't important. "I'm sorry. I still don't understand what you're talking about."

"There's something very familiar about you. Don't you feel it?"

Ron recalled his initial impression of her. His head tilted down, and he stared at the white and crimson Persian rug.

"You do."

"You're right. I do. But it's only because you remind me so much of my wife." He paused. "I miss her so much." He looked into her eyes. "You don't want to be with someone who's thinking of someone else."

She looked away. A few seconds later, she reached and grabbed the remote that was on the end table. She turned the TV off. "Then why are you here?"

"Until five minutes ago, I thought I knew." He looked at her. "Now, I'm not so sure." He was still surprised that she had come on to him. He wanted to change the topic to anything but him. He got up and knelt in front her.

"What are doing?" She said as he gently pulled up one of her sleeves.

He ran a finger along her scar. "Tell me about this."

"You already know."

"I know what Mike has told me but . . ."

"He doesn't deserve to know anything else. I don't want anything from him, unless it's his life."

"You don't mean that."

She looked away as tears welled in her eyes. "I don't know anymore." She covered her eyes as she wept. "I just miss my sister."

Ron stood up and resumed his seat next to her. He held her while she cried. The emotion was contagious. "I know."

"I believe you," she whispered.

Her reaction reminded him of Carly. He wondered what made him so believable. If she could see inside, she'd see that he was as scared, scarred and uncertain as she was. But now, she had to be his focus. "Let me help you."

"How?"

"I want to take it all away, the pain, the anger, the resentment."

"No one can do that."

Ron glanced down at the floor, then back at her. He remembered why Mike had asked him to travel to New York. "You can. Let me help you."

"Ron, that doesn't make any sense."

"I think it will, but you need to let go a little bit."

"Let go?" She stood up. "How do you just let go? Have you let go of your wife?"

The unwelcomed analogy left Ron speechless.

"It's not that easy, is it?"

"Nor should it be."

"Then what are you talking about? You're asking me to do something you haven't even done yourself. Do you think there's a difference between us just because your scars are hidden and I wear mine on my wrists?"

"The difference is in how we choose to handle each day."

"And yesterday you tried to commit suicide. Now you're all better?"

"Better than I was yesterday, yes. A lot has happened in the past twenty-four hours. I've done a lot of thinking. One step at a time, you can do the same."

"Don't get too high on your self-righteousness because when the feelings return to haunt you, you'll be looking for a way out fast."

Ron slowly shook his head. He understood that she'd been living with her pain for years. He wished he could call upon his counseling skills and find a way to help her. He reflected on what he'd lived through over the past 24 hours. "Then change your focus."

"My focus?"

"Choose to change your focus so you have something new to concentrate on, not just the past."

"But that's all I have left of her," Naomi said. "That's where she lives."

"No."

"That where your wife lives too."

"They don't *live*!" Ron screamed. Her words reminded him of what Mike had said yesterday. He got up and put his hands on her shoulders. "Don't you get it? All we have are memories. We cherish those, but we need to keep living. We need to stop searching for someone else to blame. We need to move on."

"I don't want to just move on."

"Is this how Helen would want you to live the rest of life?"

Naomi's eyes flashed between Ron's and other points in the room as if she were looking for an escape route.

"The choice is up to you. You might be punishing Mike. But even more, you're punishing yourself."

"I have no choice."

"You have whatever you believe you have."

"Then I . . ." She fell silent.

"Choose. Have faith and choose to stop hating and move on."

She fell into his arms and held onto him. "I want to, but I can't."

He held onto her. "You can."

"I'm weak."

"I'll carry you."

"You already carry too much." Tears landed on Ron's shirt as she clung to him all the more and pressed her head against his shoulder. "I don't know."

Ron was surprised at the inner strength he was feeling. "I do. I do know," he whispered.

After a minute, she gently pushed away from him and sat down.

"I'll go get us some water," Ron said. He walked into the small kitchen. After locating two glasses, he filled them with tap water. He stood in front of the sink for a moment to think. He waited for an idea or inspiration to come, but none did. He walked back into the room and handed a glass to Naomi who took a sip.

"What now?" She asked.

He smiled. "Why don't you tell me?"

"I don't think I can let Mike get away with what he did."

"I doubt he feels like he's getting away with anything." Ron sat next to her. "Just talk to him. He'll listen."

Ron knew he'd have to be strong enough for both of them. He prayed he could live up to the task.

Her stare fell toward the floor. "You make it sound so simple."

"I don't mean to, because I know it isn't. I've started one day at time, actually, minute by minute."

She looked at him with tired eyes and nodded.

"If I go find Mike, will you give him a chance?"

"I'm not promising anything."

Ron fished his phone out of his pocket. "Give me your number, and I'll call you when I find him."

Naomi gave him her number. He left his with her as well.

"I'll give him a call first," Ron said as he looked up Mike's number in his phone.

"I know where he is."

"You do?"

"There's a coffee shop at the end of street. Sometimes when . . . well, he's there. Let's just leave it at that. Just take a right when you leave the building. You'll recognize the place when you see it."

Ron wondered what the rest of the story was, but he was grateful for the direction. He smiled at her and was still surprised at how attractive she was. He hadn't thought about a woman that way since Anne had died.

Chapter 19

Coffee and a Call

Ron walked to the door and opened it. "You'll be okay until I call?"

She looked at him and nodded.

After a moment, he forced a smile. "Okay." He closed the door behind him, walked down the steps and out the main door.

The fall air was invigorating, but crisp, which made him appreciate his sport coat. He felt a new sense of purpose.

A taxi sped down the street and its brakes squealed as it approached a stop sign.

Ron descended the stairs from the entryway and turned right. He stepped out of the way to allow an older woman who was walking a white poodle to pass from the opposite direction. She eyed Ron suspiciously and held a black purse close to her fur coat as she passed. The poodle tried to stop to sniff Ron's shoe, but the woman tugged his leash. "No, Fifi Higgins. Stop that."

Ron smiled, amused at the name.

He walked to the end of the block and saw the place. At the street level of an aged, three-story brick building was a coffee shop. A sign over the windows of the establishment read, *Java Jerry's*. Ron crossed the street and squeezed through the entrance as a young couple was exiting. He saw the back of Mike's head at the booth farthest from the entrance.

The stained planks of the floor protested with faint groans as he crossed it. He slid into the seat across from Mike.

Mike continued to stare out the window and ignored Ron's presence. An untouched cup of coffee was set in front of him.

"How are you doing?" Ron finally asked.

Mike closed his eyes and slowly shook his head.

A waiter in a white shirt and tan pants stopped by the table and, in a Jamaican accent, asked what he wanted. Ron asked for coffee, black.

When the waiter left, Mike smirked. "Just like my soul," he mumbled.

"Pardon?"

"My soul. It's black." Mike's eyebrows raised and fell. "I suppose it should be since I seem to be the touch of death on peoples' lives."

"Don't blame yourself for things outside your control."

"Naomi does. Maybe she should."

"I talked to her for a while. I think she's ready to talk with you."

"I no longer know what I wanted to say to her."

The waiter served the coffee and asked if the men were getting anything to eat. Ron asked to give them a few minutes.

"How about listening? Just listen to her. I think she wants to get some stuff off her chest."

Mike continued to stare out the window. "I can't believe she tried to kill herself." Ron noticed he looked genuinely shocked. Mike looked at Ron. "And you too." He said quietly, but not in a manner that suggested surprise.

"I have no defense. I guess you showed up at the right time. Give yourself some credit."

A man in a dark blue, pinstriped suit walked past outside. It made Ron curious about Mike's old job.

"What did the two of you discuss after I left?" Mike asked.

"Life. Moving on. Stuff like that."

"Moving on," Mike echoed. He started rapidly tapping fingers on the table. "Do you think she's ready for that?"

"Not completely. But I think she took the first step. I suggested each of us move on one day at a time."

"What now?"

"I told her I'd call once I found you. She said you'd be here."

Mike flashed a smile that quickly fled. "We used to come here all the time."

Ron saw the smile tease its way back onto Mike's face. But after a few seconds, it faded again.

"I met Helen in college. At the time, it felt like one of those chance encounters you see in the movies. In hindsight, I like to think of it as two people who were destined to find each other. We met shortly after another girl dumped me." He shrugged. "I never did find out why. That's one of the hardest things for a guy like me to deal with. I'm so analytical." Mike clenched his fists. "I just have to know. But it can be impossible to know what a person's thinking. It was during a weekend trip here when I met Naomi." He shook his head. "I don't think she was too happy to see her sister with someone. She wanted Helen for herself. Yet, she was the one who moved to New York first. She actually came-on to me. I turned her down. I think she was used to getting who she wanted."

"You two started on the rocks?"

"For me and Helen, it started well, but not so much for Naomi. I think she was initially jealous. Like I said, she even threw herself at me once early on."

Ron thought about Naomi's come-on.

"I later told her she could blame the alcohol." He laughed, but the laughter died as his face became more somber. "At this point I think anything positive she ever may have felt for me is gone. And I don't just mean in a romantic sense, I mean in any sense."

Ron thought about his time with Naomi. "Let's invite her over here."

"Only if she's unarmed," Mike joked.

"Why don't I call her, and we'll have coffee."

Mike feigned a smile. His focus returned toward the other side of the window, his thoughts returning to happier times.

Ron called Naomi's number. There was no answer, and it went to voice mail. He shook his head and recalled.

"Problem?"

"No. I'm calling her now." Ron heard Naomi's voice.

"Hey."

"Hi Naomi, it's Ron."

"You found Mike?"

"Just where you said. You can join us now."

Silence.

Ron glanced at the screen to see if the call was still connected. The seconds ticked. He put the phone by his ear and heard the sound of wind. "Naomi, are you on your way?"

"There's been a change of plans."

Ron closed his eyes and sighed. "Naomi, you said—"

"I said I couldn't promise you anything."

Ron looked at Mike who had folded his arms against his chest. Ron could see Mike's jaw clenching.

"Are you still at your apartment? We can come back over."

"I'm walking over to the Liberty Cruises pier. Tell Mike if he still wants to talk, we're doing it on *my* terms on the next boat out. You guys can find me at Cindy's near Liberty Cruises. Tell Mike. He knows where it is. It's his call now."

"I'll tell him." Ron waited for a reply. "Hello?" He checked his phone only to find that the call had ended. He looked at Mike. "She hung up."

"This was a bad idea."

"You didn't think so yesterday."

"That was yesterday."

"You had a good plan."

Mike shook his head.

"Listen. You said you needed a friend to stand by you, and I agreed to that, so let's do this. She's over at Cindy's by some cruise place."

"Liberty Cruises?"

"Yeah, that's it."

Mike smirked. "Naomi used to tease me about that."

"What are these places?"

"Cindy's is a pub near Liberty Cruises. Their boats take tourists up and down the Hudson."

"What size boats?"

"They probably hold a couple hundred people. Big enough, but I've never been . . ." Mike paused. "Forget it."

"Mike, just say it."

Mike hesitated as his focus returned to outside of the window. "I've never been comfortable on the water," he said in a whisper. He looked around as if he were concerned someone might be listening to the conversation.

"And these boats sink often?" Ron asked in a joking manner. He hoped to disarm Mike enough to agree to meet Naomi. If he could at least get them together, he could help facilitate a dialogue.

"She just wants to terrorize me."

"Then let her. Once she gets everything off her chest, maybe the two of you can reconcile."

"You don't know her. She's tough as nails. Tougher."

Ron recalled his brief discussion with Naomi after Mike had left. He felt like she had exposed her vulnerable side and was wounded. As impossible as the situation seemed, he felt like he needed to help them begin the healing process.

"Mike, Naomi feels alone since losing her sister. She's frightened. She's looking for someone to blame." The words reminded Ron of what he had back home. Nothing. He fought to suppress the feelings for now. *Focus, Ron, focus.*

Ron waited for a reply but none came. He leaned in. "If you want to visit Pity City for a while, fine. But don't live there. Either *we* are going over to that pub or I'm on the next flight back to Toledo. Which is it?" He saw Mike's jaw clench again as his eyes tracked a biker with an orange backpack.

Mike looked at Ron and replied grimly, "You win. Let's get a cab."

"Can't we just walk from here?"

"The time would be about the same in this traffic."

Ron thought the traffic looked moderate but nowhere near as heavy as it was earlier that morning.

"And I don't feel like walking."

Mike scooted out of the booth, pulled out his wallet and left a twenty on the table. Without waiting for Ron, he turned and walked toward the exit.

Ron got up as the waiter arrived.

"Is there a problem, man?" The waiter asked.

"Something came up and we need to go." He tapped next to the twenty on the table. "Keep the change."

"Right on, thanks, man."

Ron exited and saw Mike climbing into a cab. He jogged the few feet over to the cab and climbed in. "Thinking of leaving without me?" He pulled the door shut.

Mike ignored Ron. "Know where Cindy's is by the Liberty Cruises?" He asked the cabby.

"Sure."

"Take us there please."

"Okay."

"Shouldn't take but five minutes. Ten minutes if he drives like a sane person," Mike said while his expression remained melancholy.

"Tell me about this stalking business Naomi says you have."

"Had."

"What were you, a P.I. or something?"

"Are you trying to change the subject?"

"I didn't know we were on one."

Mike turned his head toward the window. "I suppose you deserve to know. Like I told you yesterday, I was a data analyst. My company worked mostly with hedge funds, but also with businesses that had reams of data but weren't sure how to use it. We wrote sophisticated software that found patterns which could predict behaviors."

"I see."

"Really?"

"Finding patterns doesn't seem too complex. When I fly I see them all the time in nature, in waves and mountains. I'm not sure they're explainable like a bunch of numbers, but I think intuitively patterns are there."

"You'd be surprised. I think they can all be boiled down to numbers. Everything you see in these new video games and CGI movies is created with numbers. It's the same in nature."

"Nature is just numbers?"

"To me, everything is data."

Ron reflected on Naomi's earlier tantrum. "Even people?"

Mike hesitated for a few seconds. "Sounds cold, doesn't it."

"Maybe because it is."

"That's not my perspective. And if the truth is cold, so be it."

"But you have to empathize with how other people see it."

Mike nodded. "When I lost Helen, that was my weakness. I've been working on it ever since. Trying to make up for it. Trying to make a difference."

"How so?"

Mike glanced at Ron. He hesitated before finally speaking. "Like Naomi said, people aren't data, but I think everything we do can be quantified. I'm using that and finding ways to help people."

Ron nodded even though he couldn't fully fathom what Mike was talking about. He thought about Mike's analytics specialty. "I need to ask you something. If you're some computer whiz, how on earth did you end up at a small airport in the middle of nowhere?"

Before Mike had a chance to reply, the cab screeched to a halt.

"Cindy's Pub," the cabby said.

Chapter 20

Lunch at Cindy's

Mike reached into his back pocket and retrieved his wallet. "Can we discuss that later," he said as he fished out the cab fare.

"Just give me the summary."

Mike handed cash to the cabby. "Keep the change." He looked at Ron. "Summary, huh?" He motioned for them to get out of the cab.

"Thanks, guy," the cabby said.

Ron got out and Mike followed.

"Based on what you said back at Naomi's, showing up at your airport when I did was pretty lucky for both us. What else do you need to know?"

Motion from inside one of the pub windows caught Ron's attention. It was Naomi waving them in. "Never mind," Ron said. "Your biggest fan is waving at us."

The two men walked to the entrance, which was covered overhead with a brown awning. The name *Cindy's* was stenciled in old English lettering on the front of the awning. Ron opened the door for Mike and followed him in. He still wanted more details on Mike's background. He felt Mike was hiding something and suspected it may have something to do with the man's computer skills. He filed away the issue for future thought and looked around the pub as they walked toward the table where Naomi was seated.

"Cool place," Ron said. The pub had a brick floor that looked to date back to the founding of the country. The tables and chairs were rough sawn wood, stained dark with a hard, glossy finish.

The two men sat across from Naomi at a table adorned with a couple plastic beer ads and condiments. Ron adjusted his chair a few times until the legs sat even on the floor.

"First time here?" Naomi said to Ron.

"They don't let us out of the state too often," Ron said.

Mike nervously looked at Naomi, then grabbed one of the upright drink ads from the middle of the table and studied it as if he might be reading a book.

"What can I get you guys?" The cheerful waitress asked as she set a plate with a sandwich in front of Naomi.

"I'll have what she's having," Ron said.

"Same here," Mike added.

"And to drink?"

"Coke, Pepsi, whatever you have," Ron said.

The waitress looked at Mike who nodded. "Two Cokes it is." She disappeared as quickly as she had shown up.

"What are you guys, twins?" Naomi said.

"I'm not that hungry," Mike said.

Naomi took a bite of her sandwich. "Well," she said as she chewed. "This is the best sandwich in the whole city. Best Rueben in New York, right, Mike?"

"Sure."

"You'll have to bring your friend back here some night," she said to Mike. "They have the best imports on tap."

Ron noticed she actually smiled, but just a little. "Thanks for meeting us here."

"I couldn't resist the free lunch. Right, Mike?"

Mike nodded. "Sure."

"Ron, you'll want to try everything on the menu because Mike's got the tab. I bet he could even plug the whole menu into a computer and tell you what kind of dreams you'll have two weeks from now based on what you eat today."

Mike looked out the window toward the pier across the street. "That's enough."

"It was your idea to meet."

Ron looked Naomi in the eye. "Naomi, please. Let's just have a polite conversation."

"What are you, some kind of shrink?"

"Something like that."

"Really?"

"I have a clinic back in Ohio where I'm a family counselor."

Naomi was about to take another bite, but her hands slowly lowered the sandwich on the plate. "Isn't this just perfect. How long have you two known each other?"

"Would you believe just two days," Ron said.

"I would. Because I doubt you'd be able to stand this guy much longer than a week."

"Give it a rest already," Mike said. His focus remained out the window.

"It's okay," Ron said. "I told Naomi you'd hear her out."

Naomi's eyes alternated between the two men. She looked at Ron. "I don't know what you did to this guy, but I'll have to give you credit. He'd normally be out of here by now."

"Why's that?"

"He can't stand me."

"Do you give him a chance?"

Naomi rolled her eyes. She looked out the same window as Mike, then back at Ron. "I told you I would, so I will after lunch."

"Thank you," Ron said.

For the next few minutes, Mike's gaze remained on the world outside the restaurant. Ron glanced over at him and thought the man looked like someone who was about to have his last meal.

"Here you go, gentlemen," the waitress said as she set the plates and two drinks in front of them. She waited for a reply, but since none came, she asked if she could bring anything else. Ron said they were set for now.

Ron took a bite of the sandwich. "You're right. This is good."

"Told ya," Naomi said. "Mike, eat your sandwich. You'll need it for the cruise."

Mike ignored her.

She said to Ron, "He used to talk more. Is he always this quiet now?"

"It is good, Mike," Ron said.

Naomi and Ron continued to eat their sandwiches and after a minute, Mike finally picked his sandwich up and took a bite. For the next few minutes, the only sounds at the table were three people eating lunch. The building silence made Ron feel awkward.

Naomi finished first. She took a few drinks from her glass then got up. "I'll meet you guys at the pier. Mike, you buy the tickets. Once we're on the boat, I'll listen." She walked away and wove her way between the tables as she exited.

"That was easy," Ron joked.

Mike looked at him, then at his sandwich before taking another bite. Over the next few minutes, the two men ate their sandwiches and for the first time, Ron wished Mike would talk.

"Should we head over?" Ron said.

"I've waited two years for this. A few minutes longer won't matter."

"She might take off."

Mike pursed his lips and nodded.

"About this data business you had: did you walk away from that after you lost Helen?"

Mike looked away as if he wanted to avoid the topic. "Can we not talk about that?"

"Yesterday, you wanted to talk all the time, and I was the quiet one."

Mike almost laughed.

"What did you do when you left New York?"

"I, uh," Mike shrugged. "I guess you could say I did some traveling."

"I could, but your body language tells me there's more to it than that."

"There is, but I'm not ready to talk about that just now." Mike rotated his glass on the table. Condensation from it left a small puddle on the table and got his fingers wet. "Helen's death haunted me. I just wanted to get away."

Ron slowly nodded. "Yeah."

"So I moved around a bit."

"Okay."

"I know I'm not giving you much, but I'd like to just leave it at that, okay?"

"No, it's not okay. You're hiding something."

"I can't do this anymore." Mike leaned his elbows on the table and cradled his head in the hands.

Ron saw he was losing ground. "All right. Let's go get the boat tickets." He started to push his chair out.

Mike grabbed Ron's forearm. "You don't understand how much I hate the water." He lowered his voice and said. "It's my worst fear. I'm scared of drowning."

Ron felt a tremor in Mike's grip. He waited. After a few seconds, Mike's grasp loosened and his hand fell away. "It'll be fine, Mike. I promise. Run the numbers. How many have drowned on one of these boat cruises."

Mike shrugged. He looked at Ron with uncertainty and kept fidgeting with his glass. "Well, none."

"Case closed." Ron stood up and put his hand on Mike's shoulder. "I'll be there with you the whole time."

"Why are you doing this?"

"Because I promised you I would."

"You don't need to do this anymore."

"Listen. We're friends now and friends help each other through tough times. And as you found out this morning, I'm in debt to you. I owe you one."

"You don't know me well enough to mean that."

"Maybe not. But friends accept each other as they are. Now let's face what's in front of us."

"What's in front of us?"

"Two things. One, some release for Naomi. And two, a reprieve from her hatred toward you. But I don't think she really hates you. She just can't let go of her sister."

Mike nodded with a resigned sigh.

"Good. Let's go."

Chapter 21
On Troubled Water

Naomi had been texting on her phone but shoved it into her purse when she spotted the two men approaching. "Ready?"

"I'll get the tickets," Mike said.

"I already bought tickets, didn't want to keep you waiting any longer than necessary. The next boat leaves in a few minutes." She turned and entered the pier. Ron and Mike followed.

"Is she being sarcastic?" Mike whispered.

"I'm not sure. But let's give her the benefit of the doubt. We all want the same thing."

"Tell me again, what does she want?"

Ron smiled. "Right now, just to see you suffer through this boat ride. But longer term, she wants closure."

"Have I told you about my fear of water?"

"Many times. We'll be fine."

"Right."

The boat was much larger than Ron had expected. He estimated it was at least a hundred and fifty feet long. There were two levels. The front and back sections of the upper deck were exposed with no covering. The upper deck covered the lower deck, which was lined with large windows and rows of bench seating. There was an ad placed at eye-level that listed drinks sold from the on-board bar. The ship was painted white, although a few rust-stained runs marred the paint. The name of the company, *Liberty Cruises*, was painted in large blue letters on the side of the ship.

Naomi bounded across the short gangway and onto the boat.

"Go ahead, Mike," Ron said.

Mike paused at the foot of the gangway. He looked at Ron who nodded for him to proceed. After slowly putting his full weight on one foot onto the gangway, Mike took a second step. He took a deep breath and a few more steps, which brought him on board. Ron followed.

"Where is everyone?" Mike asked.

Ron surveyed the area. "I guess there aren't too many tourists in October." He estimated there were only a few dozen people on board. In the summer months, it was probably packed.

A deep voice over the loudspeaker announced that departure was in five minutes.

"That guy sounds like he could be a pilot," Ron said.

Mike didn't reply.

Ron saw Naomi standing at the bow. "Naomi looks relaxed. Let's head over."

"I'd rather go to the upper deck. It's further away from the water."

"But Naomi's over there," Ron pointed.

"Exactly."

"You can't avoid her forever."

"Want to bet?" Mike walked over to the stairway and walked up.

Ron walked over to Naomi and leaned on the railing next to her. She slid closer to him so that their shoulders touched.

"You got him on a boat." Ron sighed.

"Yup."

"He just went upstairs."

"Tell him to come back down. It'll be easier for me to push him off from here."

Ron laughed. "You don't mean that."

Naomi glanced over at Ron and smiled for an instant.

A voice over the loudspeaker said the tour was starting and that landmarks would be pointed out as they traveled. The engines increased in speed and the boat slowly left the pier.

Once the ship was underway and in the middle of the Hudson River, the passengers had a full view of the city and the skyline. Ron admired the view. "This would be great at night."

"It is. They have a dinner cruise I highly recommend." Naomi bumped his shoulder. "Want to take me?"

"You're pretty direct."

"A girl in the city has to go after what she wants."

Ron watched the bow wave and the patterns in the small waves generated by the ship. "I don't think the timing is quite right."

"Can I buy you a drink?"

"Would you mind getting one for Mike?"

"I'll get him one later. I left the arsenic at home."

Ron sighed. "Naomi, he agreed to your terms, which is why we're here."

"So?"

"It'd be nice if you'd talk to him before the cruise ended. He's waiting."

Naomi laughed. "He's not waiting, he's shaking. I bet he's huddled in the fetal position between the chairs upstairs."

Ron turned his body to face her. "Maybe so. But he can still listen."

Naomi looked into Ron's eyes, then at the city. "Since you're the shrink, I suppose this was all your idea, setting Mike and me up like this to talk?"

"The idea was Mike's."

"Get out of here."

"Ask him."

"I will. In his condition right now, he won't be able to lie. Getting him on the water is like giving him an injection of truth serum."

"Be nice."

"I'm harmless," she flirted.

"Uh-huh. I'll wait here."

"Sure you won't be bored?"

"With this view of New York? Not a chance. And I can always check my email."

Naomi shook her head. "You professional types. Always tethered to the office. Throw your phone in the river and relax for once."

"Mike's waiting."

Naomi glanced over as she walked away. "Don't go anywhere."

Naomi reached the top of the stairs and looked for Mike. About a dozen tourists were standing along the railing near the front of the boat in the open area. There was an older couple seated and holding hands. In the covered section, she spotted Mike sitting in a chair that was in the center of the area. She rolled her eyes and approached him with two glasses in her hand.

Mike looked up at her for a flash then continued his blank stare forward. His arms were crossed as if a straitjacket bound him.

"Would you believe they sell single malt Scotch," Naomi said matter-of-factly.

Mike didn't budge or react.

Naomi set a glass on the chair next to him. "This will help calm your nerves." She walked down the row and sat in a window seat and sipped her drink. "It's got a strong peaty aroma about it, don't you think?" She could see Mike still hadn't touched his drink. "They didn't have any cheese. Smoked cheddar would've been good with this." She took another sip. "Maybe some crackers, too."

After a few minutes, she got up and sat so that there was an empty chair between her and Mike. The glass of Scotch still remained on the chair. "Mike, when was the last time I got you anything?"

He looked at her. Her lips formed a partial smile.

"I don't know how your friend did it, but here we are on a boat in the middle of the Hudson, and I'm willing to talk. He said you'd be willing to listen."

Mike closed his eyes and held them tightly shut, anticipating the fury she was about to release.

"Well, you've got the listening part down." She paused and looked toward the city. The buildings slid by as the ship glided through the water.

"I thought a lot about what Ron said after you left my apartment. I didn't want to believe him because I figured it was just a ploy by you to manipulate me. But he made sense." She looked up and around. "I can't believe that stranger from Ohio made sense to me."

Naomi watched Mike for some indication that he was listening to her. She picked up the glass next to him and put it in his hand. He gripped it tightly with both hands.

"It's a shame you don't like boating. There's something relaxing about being on the water. To me, it's the only time when I feel like I've left my problems somewhere else.

Mike's eyes glanced toward her a few times. "That's what Ron said."

"He's a boater?"

"He said that about flying, that he likes flying because he can leave his problems back on the ground."

Naomi cringed. "It gets you from A to B, but flying isn't what it used to be."

"He has a Cessna. I meant when he flies the Cessna, not commercial flying."

"Oh."

The older couple walked from the uncovered area toward Mike and Naomi until they came to the stairs. The gentleman wore blue pants with a coat a few shades darker. His wife walked gingerly with dress shoes that were designed for form more than function. Her dress slacks were recently pressed and her crocheted sweater looked as delicate as she did.

Naomi smiled when she saw the man supporting his wife as they slowly descended the stairs. "Did you see that elderly couple? When Helen and I were teenagers, we thought that was the cutest thing. An old man would be helping his wife as they walked or something, and we both thought that was how we wanted to end up when we were that age." She looked down and her eyes scanned the floor. She took a sip of her drink. "I guess we both missed out on that."

"It'll happen for you someday, if you let it."

"Is that what your computer told you?"

"No, it's what Helen used to say."

Naomi frowned. "She's not here to defend herself, so don't you go putting words in her mouth."

"Once you find someone you can trust-"

Naomi interrupted him. "I can't trust. People lie. They're all liars." She paused. "I'm better off this way."

Mike lifted his drink but only inhaled the aroma. "I'm not." His hand settled back into his lap still holding the untouched beverage. "I'm not better off."

"You mean without Helen?"

"She was a part of me, well, a part of both you and me . . . that we'll never have again." His head dropped and he slowly shook it. "I miss her so much."

Naomi's lip quivered as she looked at him. Her breathing increased and she gripped the glass in her hand so hard it would have broken if the glass weren't as thick as it was. Her eyelids flickered. "And you think I don't miss her," she said curtly.

Mike suddenly downed his drink. He slammed the empty glass against the plastic chair seat. Naomi shuddered at the sound.

"Of course you do," Mike said. "And it's my fault. I should have seen it coming. But who can expect that of his own brother?"

Mike looked at her profile. She didn't turn to face him. "So blame me. Blame me until the end of time if it makes you feel better. But it's not going to bring her back. I've been living like an amputee since she died."

She looked at him for a few moments, and then focused forward again. She downed the last of her drink.

He reached over to touch her hand, but as he did she pulled away.

"I don't want to live like this any longer," she said.

"You want me to jump off the boat?"

"That's not what I mean." She looked at him. "Then again, maybe you should jump off the boat."

"Would that bring Helen back? Would that make you feel better?"

She looked away. "Ron said something to me. Something about letting go."

"He did?"

She closed her eyes and nodded. "He said to move on." She set her empty glass on the chair beside the glass Mike had emptied. "It sounded so easy."

"Sounds like good advice."

"Of the three of us: you, me and Ron. I think you're the only one who's done it."

"I'm trying."

"Maybe it's easier when you're analytical."

"Maybe."

Naomi crossed her arms. "But that's not me. I can't forget her so easily."

Mike twisted his body to face Naomi. A look of astonishment possessed his face. "Easy?" His eyes grimaced with pain. "You think it's easy for me to go on like this?"

"That's not what I meant."

"It's what you said."

Naomi threw her hands up. "Then maybe it is what I meant! You left the city right after her funeral. All you ever told us was that you were 'going west,' whatever that meant. Probably taking your stalking business somewhere else."

Mike shook his head. "That's not what happened."

Naomi's jaw locked. "It's what I saw." She got up. "If that's not what happened, then what *did* happen?"

Mike looked at her. "What difference does it make?"

"Plenty."

"Really?"

Naomi sat back down and shrugged. "Maybe." She turned her body to face him. "Try me."

Mike sighed. "A couple months before my crazy brother did what he did, I was approached by some people who offered me a job."

"Did this new job have something to do with Helen's death?"

"No." Mike looked at the floor. "Actually, it might have prevented it."

"What do you mean?"

Mike glanced at Naomi and saw her cross her arms. "They were from a non-profit organization that wanted to use data analysis to try and predict behavior."

"Yeah, yeah, that's what you were already doing for companies or hedge funds or whatever."

"This was different, very different. They wanted me to write software that could analyze the events that were going on in a person's life including things at work, at home, how happy they were and a huge list of other variables to analyze and predict behavior."

"That sounds awfully personal. How were you supposed to do that?"

"Ever hear of the internet?"

Naomi glared at him.

"First I should tell you *why* they wanted this information."

"Whatever it was, I'm sure it's bad."

Mike shook his head. He looked into her eyes. "They wanted to prevent suicides."

Naomi winced. "How? I mean how on earth can you write a program for that?"

Mike flashed a smile.

Naomi's eyes widened. "Wait. You actually wrote one?"

He nodded.

"How?"

Mike looked down at the floor again and sighed. "You're not going to like it."

"Wait a minute. You actually figured out how to fix your stalking software so that it could do something good for the world?"

"It's data analysis, not stalking," he said in exasperation.

She leaned back in the seat and shook her head. "I don't like it. I love it!" She leaned toward Mike and touched his arm. "Mike, that's amazing. And you're telling me it actually works?"

"Oh, yes."

She frowned. "Why would you think I wouldn't like it?"

"Because of all the personal data that has to be gathered."

Naomi looked at him inquisitively.

"The only way I could make it work was to gather everything, and I mean everything, that I could to figure out how high of a risk the person was. It meant I had to track the person's Internet activity and monitor their emails and their activities on social networking sites. A few times, we even hired private investigators who discovered specific details." He looked at her for a reaction. "I know it doesn't sound ethical, but I believed the end justified the means." He looked away. "I still do."

Naomi looked forward. "I have mixed feelings about this."

"Many of us did until we saw the results."

"What were they?"

"We batted a thousand."

"Impossible. Maybe the people in your test group or control group or whatever you call it weren't really that much at risk."

"They were."

"How do you know?"

"Because." He swallowed. "Because to verify that the software was working, we tracked two groups of people we rated the same risk."

"And?"

"And the suicide attempt rate for the control group we ignored was over sixty percent. We prevented suicides for everyone in the group we didn't ignore."

"Oh-" Naomi covered her mouth.

"Yeah, exactly. How do you walk away from something that can help so many people even though you know it's ethically dubious?" He looked at Naomi and saw she was deep in thought.

"This is how you met Ron," she said bluntly.

"In so many words, yes."

"It's not how you met Ron?"

Mike nodded. "The software did identify Ron as high risk."

"There's something you're not telling me. What was the deal with that conversation about the gun?"

Mike was silent for a few moments. "I sabotaged it."

"You sabotaged the gun?"

"Until he told me that it fired, I thought I had."

"How?"

Mike shrugged. "Put simply, I snuck into his house when he wasn't home and bent the part of the trigger or firing pin, whatever you call it, that makes the bullet fire."

Naomi, wide eyed, shook her head. "Unbelievable."

He glanced at her. "I guess I was just lucky it didn't fire initially."

"He certainly was. And then?"

"Based on my software, I figured his next attempt would be in his airplane." He shrugged again. "So I met him at the airport when he got there."

"But how? How you could possibly know?"

"I told you. My software. It works."

Naomi starred in disbelief.

"Let me get this off my chest."

"What?"

"You were right about my brother, and I didn't see it."

Naomi recoiled in her seat. She shook her head. "Don't tell me the software told you he was going to do something bad and you ignored it."

"No, it wasn't designed for that. But later, I was curious if I could write similar software to predict violent behavior." He saw that Naomi's breathing had suddenly increased. She held her crossed arms tightly against her chest. "It said he was within a ninety percent probability."

Naomi choked. "I hate you."

"Naomi, it was after the fact."

"But you could have prevented it."

"No. No, I couldn't. That's like saying you could prevent a plane crash by never letting another plane take off."

"That doesn't make sense."

"What I mean is that once you change what's going on, the person's behavior will somehow be changed from the point when you interfere."

"Helen would still be alive if someone had interfered." A caustic laugh escaped from Naomi's mouth as she looked away from him. "I told you. You idiot, I told you he was dangerous. I didn't need any software for that." She slowly shook her head. "Sometimes you just need to open your eyes, Mike. You just refused to see what was right in front of you."

The sound of the ship's horn filled the air. A fainter horn sounded a few seconds later. A similar tour boat going the opposite direction passed a few hundred yards away.

"You're right," Mike whispered. "I should have listened." He looked at her and saw she appeared to be deep in thought again.

"You've been doing this ever since you left the city?"

"I also did more solitary jobs that let me drive around and travel a lot. Courier, truck driver, delivery for a short while. Stuff like that. It all ran together." He looked away from her and watched the other boat pass by. "Ever since I lost Helen, I've been trying to do good things to try and make up for it."

"It's not just a hole you can fill."

"So I've found out."

She got up. "This is all really weird. I need some air." She walked toward the open area of the upper deck.

Chapter 22

Three Coffees

Ron noticed a few of the people around him had coffee, soda, or beer. More so than when the cruise had begun. The river breeze increased his desire for something warm. He pushed away from the railing and walked toward the enclosed lower deck.

As he passed a stairwell, his peripheral vision saw someone falling toward him. Instinctively, he braced one foot back and broke the fall of the woman who had lost her footing. They both toppled to the ground, and the elderly woman landed on top of Ron.

"Rosie!" Ron heard the elderly gentleman exclaim with alarm.

"Oh," she said. "I'm, oh my . . ."

People in the vicinity rushed over. Some of them leaned over her or knelt down. Ron heard offers for help directed toward the woman.

The old man who had been escorting her down the stairs came over. "Rosie, are you hurt?" He looked around with a look of desperation. "Is there a doctor on board?" Ron could hear the terror in the man's voice.

A couple of men helped the woman to her feet. She mumbled in response as they helped her. Ron could see she was confused. Two men guided her to a seat nearby where the old man quickly joined her like a mourning dove reuniting with his mate. A young man helped Ron up and asked if he was okay. Ron said he was fine, though his side hurt where the woman's elbow had landed during her fall. He walked over to the elderly couple and crouched to their eye level.

"Are you okay, ma'am?"

She looked at him with wide eyes, then to the old man.

"This man broke your fall," he explained to her. He looked at Ron. "I hope she didn't break *you.*"

Ron smiled. "No worse for the wear."

"My wife and I are in your debt."

Ron waved him off.

The old man held his wife while talking to her. "Are you all right?"

"I think . . . I think so," she replied.

"Nothing broken?"

"No, but I might not feel it until tonight or tomorrow."

The old man looked at Ron. "Ah, she's okay. Once she starts joking with you, you know she's fine. She looks fragile, but she's tough." He reached a hand out to Ron. "My name's Lawrence Herbert, and this here is my

Rosie." He leaned in a few inches. "I think the two of you already met."

Ron put his hand on his side. "She left an impression on me."

Lawrence scrutinized Ron's face for a few seconds then started laughing, slowly at first then into a deeper laugh. "I hope it wasn't too deep."

"I'll be fine, thank you."

"No. Thank *you.* If you hadn't been there, my Rosie here might have ended up in pieces."

Ron smiled. "Sometimes we're in the right place at the right time, but like you said, she's tough."

"Indeed, indeed," Lawrence said. He reached behind him and produced his wallet. "Here, let me give you something for your trouble."

"Oh, no," Ron said. "No trouble at all. It was a privilege."

"I'm sure a few bucks wouldn't hurt. Maybe get your wife something nice, right?"

Ron cringed. "I think, uh, that won't be necessary. Please, put your wallet away."

Lawrence hesitated for a moment then slowly slid his wallet in his back pocket.

Rosie sighed. She gently brushed at her clothes to wipe away any lose debris.

"Ma'am, how are you feeling?" Ron asked.

She slowly nodded. "I'll be okay. Thank you, young man. Thank you."

"There's a bar or café or something right over there." Ron tilted his head toward the enclosed area. He looked at Rosie. "Why don't I help you over to one of the tables?"

She smiled. "Thank you."

"You might not expect it, but their coffee is pretty good," Lawrence said.

Ron and Lawrence helped Rosie get up. The trio slowly plodded to a table in the covered area. Once the older couple was settled, Ron excused himself to get the beverages. He returned after a few minutes and set a beverage holder with three coffees on the table. "There's cream and sugar packets," Ron said as he took the packets out of the carrier and set them on the table.

"Isn't this great service, Rosie?" Lawrence said. He looked at Ron as he sat across from the couple. "I met her on one of these river cruises over 50 years ago."

Ron smiled. He took the lid off his coffee cup and sipped.

"Is your wife here?" Rosie asked. "I'd like to meet the lucky young gal."

"Now, don't be so nosy," Lawrence chided. He looked at Ron. "I'm sure when she pops up, we'll meet her."

"You say the two of you met on one of these boats?" Ron said trying to redirect the topic away from himself. He didn't want to explain his situation. He thought of his conversation earlier at Naomi's apartment and tried to take his own advice to move on.

"Oh, yes." Rosie's eyes widened like a child seeing presents under the tree for the first time. She looked at her husband in a manner that made her face glow. "He was with some boys from the Navy."

"How about that?" Lawrence said. "We got off one boat and onto another." He pointed a finger pointed toward the floor. "This one had dames." He winked.

"Oh, Lawrence." Rosie laughed. "Anyway, I saw him making time with this blonde who clearly wanted nothing to do with him."

Lawrence shook his head. "That's not how I remember it. That gal was plenty interested."

"Who's telling this story?"

"You go ahead and tell it, but tell it right," Lawrence joked.

Rosie leaned toward Ron a few inches. "Fifty years he's been trying to make himself look like a Casanova."

"I did just fine."

"Did you even get that gal's name?"

"Of course I got her name."

"What was it?"

Lawrence picked up his coffee. "Doesn't really matter now, does it."

"See?" Rosie shook her head smiling. "So like I was saying, he was . . ." She looked at her husband. ". . . with this blonde."

"That's how I remember it."

"And I saw him and actually laughed to myself just a little bit."

"She never laughed."

"I laugh all the time."

"Not on that day, you weren't laughing when me and, uh, you know, me and that blonde were talking so well."

"Okay, well, I saw the girl who was so interested in Lawrence keep looking past him toward another sailor."

"There wasn't another sailor over where she was looking."

"The boat was full of sailors."

"There weren't any where *she* was looking though."

"If you say so." Rosie gently shook her head a bit and smiled slyly. "I walked over and, this was very direct for a girl back then mind you, I walked over and asked that gal if I could talk to my friend." She nodded once. "I acted as if I knew him."

Lawrence laughed. "I took one look at her, and I knew. Like the way you know when you got the right answer to a hard question. Sometimes you just know."

She reached over and tapped Ron's arm. "Three weeks later we were married."

"Three weeks," he echoed.

Ron watched the two of them gaze adoringly at each other as if they were newlyweds.

Lawrence looked over to Ron. "I think if you're a good person, things will work out for you."

Rosie smiled at her husband. "Things sure have worked for us."

The well-intended words struck Ron with the void in his future. He took a large gulp of coffee, which burned his mouth. Involuntarily, he choked, and coffee spilled down his chin. He grabbed a napkin to catch it.

"Down the wrong pipe?" Lawrence said.

Ron glanced over at Lawrence. "Yeah, I, uh . . ." He fought the temptation to correct the couple since his own experience contradicted their theory. It also made him wonder if he was a bad person who got what he deserved. He spoke while he dried his face. "So just be good and things work out?"

"Well, of course, dear," Rosie said. She tapped her husband's arm. "Remember Harry and Monica and how they were caught lying about taking something from the A&P?"

"Oh yeah," Lawrence nodded. "They got divorced."

"Had it coming," Rosie said. "He cheated on her."

"You mean she cheated on him," Lawrence said.

"They cheated on each other. They weren't good people so that's what happened to them."

"I don't think it's that simple," Ron said. "How's that bible verse go? Something like it rains and shines on the just and unjust alike?"

"I'm not familiar with that one," Rosie said. "And I think I know the book pretty well."

"We have a bible?" Lawrence asked.

"Yes, it's that nice looking leather-bound book on the bookshelf."

"Oh, right, the brown leather book."

"That's the one."

"Nice looking book." He nodded. "Great book."

Ron reflected on the verse the preacher had read at his wife's funeral. It was a passage he'd heard at other funerals. Yet every time, it seemed so poignant. He wondered about the shepherd who guided people through the shadow of death. He felt a chill run down his spine at the thought that Mike might be a shepherd sent to help him. Ridiculous. Then again, Mike had done him no harm and made a significant impact on his life in just the past day and a half. He wondered how Mike and Naomi were doing.

"Ron, are you okay?" Rosie asked.

"Yeah, I was thinking of something."

"Tell us about it," she said.

Ron tilted his coffee cup so he could see into it. It was nearly empty. He remembered the police report he had yet to read. He felt if he simply read the report, it would be a step forward in moving on. He decided to get it over with. "If you would please excuse me, I just remembered some business I need to take care of."

"In the middle of the river?" Lawrence asked.

Ron held his phone up for an instant.

"Poor guy can't get away," Rosie said to her husband.

"Put your time in now and your future will be secure." Lawrence nodded.

Ron nearly laughed since he found Lawrence's statement questionable. In spite of all Ron had worked for, that which was most important to him had been lost in an instant. He got up. "It was nice meeting you folks."

"The pleasure was all ours," Lawrence said.

"Thank you again," Rosie said.

Lawrence shook Ron's hand, and Rosie went through the trouble to get up. She hugged and patted him on the back.

Ron noticed the area at the back of the boat was open. He walked over and sat down. He selected the email icon on his phone and tapped open the police report.

Chapter 23

So Cold

The breeze that ran over Mike's face did nothing to sooth his fears. "I need to keep the discussion going with Naomi," he whispered to himself. "I can take it. I can take anything she dishes out."

He made an effort to get up but his knees buckled as fear and anxiety pinned him to the chair. He could see people in the open area near the perimeter leaning on the railing. Naomi was alone. She was seated in the middle of the open area. The folds of her black jacket and her hair flowed with the wind. She looked so peaceful as if no turmoil could possibly exist beneath such a well-groomed surface.

Mike's jaw clenched as his hands pressed against the seat. Like someone learning to walk for the first time, he gripped the seatback in front of him to get up. "Just do this, Mike. Nothing to fear but fear itself," he kept repeating to himself. He looked around quickly to see if anyone was watching or listening.

He finally stood. His knuckles were white due to his grip on the seatbacks, which kept him steady. "Move on. Move forward," he whispered to himself. The vibrations from the boat reverberated through the seatback to his hand. He took a few deep breaths and slowly released his grip but clenched his hands at his sides.

He stood alone with nothing but with determination on his face.

Naomi looked over her shoulder when Mike tapped it. "Look who wandered into the wild blue open."

Mike sat next to Naomi. "What was it that Ron said? One step at a time or something to that effect."

"Sounds familiar."

The two of them sat together and faced forward. The wind gently brushed their faces.

"I've been thinking," Naomi said.

"Me too."

"Sure you want to do this?"

"Absolutely."

Naomi glanced over at Mike, and then looked past the young couples leaning on the railing, whispering sweet nothings to each other. The water ahead looked so serene.

"I want to get past this, but I honestly don't see how it's possible."

"I understand. I'm more to blame for what happened than anyone else. I should have paid more attention to what was going on with my brother. I looked at him through rose-colored glasses and lost my best friend because of it."

"And I lost my best friend too."

"I know, and I'm sorry. I'd do anything."

She cut him off. "You can't." She moved her arms animatedly to emphasize the words. "So don't make it sound so easy."

"You're right." Mike looked away from her and toward the floor. A discarded candy wrapper swirled with the wind between the legs of the chairs.

"I feel like I'm going in circles in my mind. I'm stuck and can't break free."

"What do you need to break free?"

"Closure."

"What can I do?"

Naomi closed her eyes. "Die."

Ron slid his finger down on the screen of his phone as he read the police report email from Sergeant Luca back home. He skipped the information at the top of the report because he didn't want to see his wife's name anywhere. He just wanted the closure that he hoped would come from reading the facts of the case.

He saw a diagram of the intersection, which had the minivan and truck icons. His eyes inadvertently saw the investigating officer's remarks, "killed instantly on impact," regarding the minivan's occupants. Ron looked up and through unfocused eyes watched the churning water behind the boat.

He looked back down to his phone. Somewhere in the report there had to be answers. He read that both drivers had their seatbelts on and that drugs or alcohol had impaired neither driver.

Why, God? Why did they have to die? He again focused on the boat's wake. He looked for patterns, signs or anything else that might give him answers.

He swiped up on the phone to get the drivers' details. He quickly scanned his wife's information, recognizing their address. The trucking company was located just south of Canton, and the driver's name was Michael Schwartz of New York.

Ron's heart skipped a beat. *Michael Schwartz of New York.* He felt his muscles contract.

"It can't be. There have to be a lot of Michael Schwartzs from New York," he told himself.

Thinking he must've misread, Ron looked over the report once more. This time he was sure to concentrate on the truck driver. It *was* Mike.

His friend.

But as of this moment, his enemy.

If revenge were best served cold, then using the chilly Hudson River to administer justice would be payback. Ron knew it wouldn't bring his family back, but it would give them justice - the same justice Sergeant Luca had already denied Ron.

Ron got up and stuffed the phone in the inside pocket of his coat. With an inner strength he hadn't felt in years, Ron quickly surveyed the few faces on the lower deck as he ran through the enclosed area toward the stairwell.

Lawrence and Rosie said something to him as he ran past them, but he didn't hear them. He reached the open area and the stairwell. As he rapidly ascended, he skipped every other step.

His sole purpose in life was to find Mike, and he would see to it Mike finally faced justice.

"Naomi, that won't bring Helen back," Mike pleaded.

"You wanted me to feel better, right?"

"I could drop dead right now, but it won't do any good."

Naomi crossed her arms. "Let's try it first," she said with a chill that would freeze hell.

"You know as well as I there's nothing anyone on earth can do to bring her back. Don't you think I would've done it if, it were possible?"

Naomi closed her eyes as she thrust her fingers through her hair in frustration. "I'm so confused." She yanked on her hair and pulled back a couple strands. "I'm so tired of carrying this burden."

Mike recognized the change in her mood, a symptom of her unpredictable condition. "Let that burden go, Naomi."

"I can't."

"Of course you can. Do you know how?" Mike watched her with expectation and excitement.

Her breathing increased and a stream of tears fell from her eyes. "I, I . . . I don't know. I feel safer living with this curse than living without it. I hate it but I'm addicted. It's my only connection to my sister." She looked into his eyes. "Help me, Mike."

Mike leaned over and did something he had never done before. He hugged the woman who hated him more than anything. And she hugged him back.

"It's okay, Naomi. Things are going to be okay now." He felt her go limp in his arms as she surrendered.

She sobbed into his shoulder. "Mike," she whispered, "I forgive you."

The instant the words hit his ears, Mike started sobbing too. "Thank you, Naomi. Thank you."

They held each other until the sound of heavy footsteps pounding up the nearby stairs interrupted them. Mike gently released Naomi and she leaned back into the chair.

"Mike!" Mike and Naomi turned and saw Ron's heaving figure coming toward them. "You murderer!" He screamed.

Everyone who had been watching the cityscape go by was now watching Ron.

Ron grabbed Mike by the lapel and threw him to the floor. Ron jumped on top of him and shook him violently. "How could you?" His voice broke as tears fell from his cheeks. "You killed my family!"

"What?" Mike said.

Ron felt the stares from the crowd. "This man killed my wife and my son," he yelled to everyone. Like a rabid dog, he was ready to attack anyone who dared to disagree with him.

Ron's face altered to one of pity. But it was pity for

himself. He looked Mike in the eyes. "I trusted you. I thought you were my friend. But you've been playing me the whole time."

"No, Ron. Listen. Listen to me."

"Why should I listen to you?"

"It was an accident. I swear it was. Check with the police."

"I saw the police report. *You* did it. *You* were the truck driver. *You* killed them."

"Yes, but the van ran the light. I never had a chance to hit the brakes."

"Murderer!"

"It was over in a flash, Ron. Please believe me."

"Never!"

"There was nothing I could do. There was nothing anyone could do." He shook his head. "I'm so sorry."

Naomi backed away from them until she was with the crowd next to the railing. She had her hands over her mouth.

"Liar!" Ron punched Mike in the face. As he pulled his other fist back to hit Mike even harder, his elbow slammed into a chair back that sent a wave of pain down his forearm.

Ron twisted as he yelped, and Mike was able to grab a post that was fastened to the deck and pull himself away so he could lift his legs. Once he did, he pushed Ron off of him. Mike scrambled to his feet and ran through the doorway into the covered area.

Ron's side, which was already sore from catching the woman earlier, fell against a chair, sending another shock of pain through his body. He pressed against the anchored chair and raised himself up. He stumbled to his feet as he fought the pain in his side.

Ron looked at Naomi with dark eyes. "Don't you worry, I'll get him. I'll get him for both of us." He was surprised to see her eyes devoid of the rage and anger he had seen in them earlier. He figured Mike must have manipulated her to believe his lies. It didn't matter.

He pursued after Mike through the covered area until there was nowhere else to go. Mike was braced against the back railing. The angry water churned in the ship's wake below.

"I thought you were my friend," Ron said.

With wide eyes, Mike stared at Ron's wretched face. "I am." He looked behind him toward the water and fell to his knees. "It was an accident. You know that, right? There was nothing I could do." His face fell.

"Naomi was right," Ron said through gritted teeth. "Everyone around you dies. You *are* the angel of death."

"No, no, no," Mike pleaded. "Please don't say that. I . . . maybe I . . ." He didn't look up. He pressed his palms against the sides of his head.

Ron's breathing remained intense as he fought the desire to grab Mike and throw him over the railing. He took a step forward to do just that when he heard Mike whisper something.

"What?"

Mike looked up. "It can't be, but, but it must be. Everyone around me dies. I can't do this to people I love. I can't let this happen to good people." He slowly got up.

He kept rising as he climbed the railing. "You're right. You and Naomi are both right. I'm sorry."

"Mike, no!" Ron heard Naomi scream. He turned and saw her running toward them. She stopped beside Ron when she saw that Mike was leaning backward. The only thing that kept him from falling was one hand grasping the railing.

"Don't do this, Mike," Naomi said.

Ron was dumbfounded. He was expecting Naomi to run forward a few more steps and push Mike into the river.

"I have to, Naomi," Mike said.

Ron saw Mike's eyes plead with his own. Ron's face remained unchanged.

Mike forced a quick smile. "It's okay. I've got to end this. Now."

"No!" Naomi screamed. She lurched forward as Mike released his hold and fell into the churning water below.

Chapter 24
Judgment

Naomi leaned over the railing and watched as Mike disappear beneath the foaming watery wake. "Do something!" She screamed at Ron. She climbed a rung on the railing and scoured the area for Mike.

Speechless, Ron looked at her while his chest heaved.

People on both decks of the boat crowded toward the rear. Murmurs swept through the small crowds as many rushed to the rear railings and peered overboard. Dozens of pairs of eyes searched the water's foamy surface.

"Isn't this what you want?" Ron said, sharply confused.

Naomi stepped off the railing toward Ron and pushed him. "He's going to die. Don't you know he can't swim?" She pounded on his chest with her fists. "Do something, damn you!"

"He can't hurt anyone anymore. It's over."

"He never did hurt anyone. I see now." She looked toward the water then back at Ron. "Don't you see? It was never his fault," she pleaded.

Ron felt the boat slow as the engines shut off.

Naomi gripped Ron's shoulders roughly and spoke to him, slowly and forcefully. "Ron. Mike is going to die unless you do something."

"Why should I help the man who killed my family?" Ron said through gritted teeth. He fought the urge to push Naomi away. He looked around at the crowd. If they only knew what he knew, they'd understand justice had been done and go about their business.

"He didn't kill your family. I heard everything. She ran the intersection. There was nothing he could do."

Ron looked past her and toward the river. He recalled the details from the accident report. "Justice has to be done."

"What about justice for the innocent?"

"My family was innocent."

"So was Mike." Naomi grabbed Ron by his shirt and shook him. "Ron, Mike's as innocent as your family."

"My fam . . ." Ron's eyes glanced upward as he saw something white flitting toward them in the sea breeze. A white dove feather briefly landed on Naomi's bangs, with a gust of wind was just as quickly whisked away. *Anne?* Was it a sign from her?

Ron quickly slipped off his coat and shoes. He took a deep breath as he leapt over the handrail.

The chilly water hit him hard and took his breath away. He cried out as he surfaced and swiped at his left eye to try and clear something from it. When he looked at his hand, he saw it was covered in blood. He coughed as the pain from his forehead struck him and he saw a floating piece of wooden debris floating a few feet away.

Naomi was leaning over the railing and scanning the surface. Nearly everyone on board was now at the back of the boat watching the unfolding drama as *man overboard* rippled through the crowd.

"Ron! Ron, are you okay?" He heard Naomi yell from the boat.

She gasped and put her hands over her mouth.

"Ron, you're hurt," she yelled. She quickly looked in both directions. "Is there a life preserver anywhere? Someone find a life preserver!" she called behind her. "Hold on, Ron!"

Ron blinked rapidly. The chilly water was already making his muscles tighten. "I need to find Mike," he hollered toward the boat.

"What?" Naomi yelled. "I can't hear you."

He looked in every direction for his friend. He concluded Mike was a couple hundred feet away since the boat had kept going after Mike had jumped. Ron made the effort to keep swimming but his body was fighting him. He tensed his arms and legs and felt some control return to his limbs. With short, choppy strokes, he swam to the area where he thought Mike would be.

"Mike," he screamed. He looked back at the ship. It wasn't in focus too well, and Ron wiped his left eye again to try to clear it. "Does anyone see him?" He hollered toward the ship.

Nothing. He wondered if anyone on the ship could hear him. Could they even see him? His head throbbed. He felt alone, and his body started to sink beneath the surface. He instinctively kicked and got his head above water. He felt his nerves twitch as a panic attack tried to set in. He choked as he inhaled some water and gasped for breath.

"Mike!" He coughed. He slowly turned his body and scanned the water. "Aghh!" He screamed as he felt something constrict around his legs. He pulled his knees up and grabbed at whatever was touching him. He yanked part of the thing above the surface and recognized the fabric. It was the sleeve of Mike's coat. His legs felt free but his arms involuntarily spasmed in the cold water. "Mike," he said with a hoarse voice and desperation. He didn't know how much longer he could tread water.

Sudden cries from the ship caught his attention, and he saw arms pointing. He followed their direction and saw something rapidly nearing - a ski boat. He tried to stick his arm up, but it was too heavy. When the boat was almost on top of him, it suddenly turned, but the bow wave swamped him. The waves went over his head, and he held his breath and bobbed up and down while trying to survive the wash.

Approximately twenty feet away, he glimpsed a hand break the surface in the receding wake of the passing ski boat. *Mike!* The hand disappeared just as quickly.

He swam over to where he'd seen the hand. "Mike," he croaked weakly.

He dove to find his friend, but in the murky water, he could only see a few yards, if that. He surfaced and yelled Mike's name again. The only thing he heard was the ski boat.

Ron took a deeper breath then dove again. This time he barely spotted Mike's lifeless body. He grabbed him and kicked hard to reach the surface. He leaned backward and held Mike's head above the water. The sound of the ski boat was getting loader. Suddenly, the engine reduced to a rumble. He saw the boat slowly approaching him.

"Here," Ron coughed. "Over here!" He yelled louder. Every few seconds he waved with his free arm. Finally, the boat pulled up beside the two men.

"Hey, man, we didn't see you at first," said the man on the ski boat. His blond hair was spiked with gel. A woman in a yellow windbreaker gripped the back of the seat next to him.

"Here, take him first," Ron said.

The young couple pulled Mike up and into the boat. Ron heard him land with a thud. Next, they helped Ron aboard.

"Mike." Ron slapped Mike's face, partially out of anger and partially with the hope of waking him. He turned Mike on his side. He pounded him on the back and water came out of his mouth. Ron pounded his back a few more times then rolled him onto his back. "Come on, man."

Mike's lifeless body started to scare Ron. He felt it was his fault Mike had jumped. He pinched Mike's nose and gave him a few breaths. He checked for a pulse, found none and started chest compressions. His arms felt like rubber.

"Wake up, man," Ron said. He gave Mike a few more breaths. "Don't you dare do this to me!" Ron screamed. He slapped Mike again. He looked up and saw the young couple staring at him. He did four more chest compressions and gave Mike a few more breaths.

Mike coughed weakly.

"Mike!"

Mike hacked repeatedly and water gushed out of his mouth. He leaned over the boat and vomited.

Ron slumped weakly against the side of the boat with relief. "That's good. Let it out. Let it all out."

Mike rolled back over and looked at Ron with anxious eyes. "You aren't going to kill me?" he whispered.

Ron slowly shook his head. "No." He reached over and gripped Mike's shoulder. "I know what happened now. I understand."

Mike looked at him in disbelief.

Ron grabbed a towel that was lying nearby and put it under Mike's head. "It wasn't your fault." He nodded and looked up at the young couple. "What happened was an accident." He looked back down at Mike. "I understand now. It was an accident."

The young man and woman looked at each other with curiosity and shrugged.

Ron pointed toward the tourist boat and breathing hard he asked, "Can you take us over to that boat?"

"Is that the one you guys were on?"

"Yes."

"Yeah, no problem." The engine roared and the ski boat accelerated toward the tourist boat. The brief jaunt was over as quickly as it had started, and the young man steered the boat so that its momentum carried it close to the back of the tourist boat. Someone from the tourist ship tossed a rope and the young man grabbed it. He slowly pulled the ski boat closer until it was against the back of the other boat's rubber rub-rail. A couple life preservers thrown into the water earlier to help the men gently tapped the ski boat's hull.

On the rear of the tourist boat, a few steps led to a landing a few inches above the surface. Naomi quickly made her way to the landing.

Ron and the man with the spiked hair helped Mike up and held him steady as they stepped onto the tourist boat.

"Here," Naomi said as she reached out and grabbed Mike's hand. She held onto the railing with her other hand. Mike looked at her in disbelief as she helped him aboard. With trembling legs, Ron followed.

The elderly couple was sitting a few rows away from the landing, and they applauded when they saw Ron. "That was incredible, just incredible," Rosie said.

"It's a shame you're married or we might have to set you up with our daughter. She's recently become available," Lawrence smiled.

Ron glanced at them but didn't react. Lawrence's comment didn't sting as much as he thought it should, and he wasn't sure just why. But right now it didn't matter. He followed Naomi, who was holding Mike up as she escorted him.

The light breeze chilled Ron through his wet clothes. Mike, he thought, must be even colder. He saw two people wearing white and blue *Liberty Cruise* jackets walking quickly toward them. The short red-haired employee's nametag read, *Darla.* The other tanned burly employee's nametag read, *Chad.* Both employees had thick blankets slung over their shoulders, and Chad was carrying a first aid kit. They were a welcome sight.

Mike collapsed into the nearest empty seat at one of the tables. Naomi sat next to him. Ron's legs gave out, and he fell into the seat across from them.

"That's quite a gash you have," Chad said to Ron as he set the first aid kit on the table.

Naomi reached for the first aid kit. "I'll take care of this."

"You must be freezing." Darla said as she wrapped Mike in a blanket.

"Thanks," Mike said through chattering teeth.

Chad offered Ron a blanket, and he wrapped himself tightly in it.

"Can I get you some coffee?" Darla asked.

Both men nodded.

"We'll bring some food, too," Chad said.

"Thank you," Naomi said.

Over the next few moments, Ron, Mike, and Naomi all traded uneasy glances. Ron heard the ship's engines restart.

Naomi was the first to finally speak. "Mike, what were you thinking?" Her hands were gripping the first aid kit.

Mike shivered in the blanket and shook his head while avoiding Ron's stare.

"Mike, I don't blame you for the accident."

"Yes, you do," Mike said softly through quivering lips.

Ron shook his head. "It was an accident. It wasn't your fault. I can accept that now."

Mike looked at Naomi who smiled weakly at him.

"I know what your brother did wasn't your fault," Naomi said.

Darla returned with hot coffees and sandwiches and set them on the table. "I can dress that wound for you," she said to Ron.

Naomi tapped the first aid kit. "Don't worry, I got it."

Darla hesitated as Naomi's fingers tapped the kit. "Let me know if there's anything else we can do to make you more comfortable. We're returning to the pier and should be there shortly."

When she left, the three of them reached for the coffees. They all sipped in unison. Naomi and Ron set their cups down on the table while Mike held his with both hands.

Naomi got up, opened the kit and began dressing the wound on Ron's forehead. "You know, Mike," she said while tending to the wound, "Ron almost lost his head going after you."

"How do you mean?" Mike asked.

"Didn't you see the debris floating in the water? Who knows how jagged it was." She put a gauze pad laced with antiseptic cream over the cut and taped it down. She kissed him on the forehead as an afterthought. "Good as new."

Ron smiled. "Amazing what a guy goes through for a kiss these days, isn't it?" He said to Mike.

Naomi smiled.

Ron saw her searching his eyes. When he looked into hers, he saw something new - peace.

A teen ran up to the table with Ron's coat and shoes. "Hey, I thought you might want these back," the guy said.

"Thank you. Just set them here."

The teenager draped the coat over the chair and set the shoes on the floor. "That was a great leap, man. With moves like that, you should be doing movies or in the Olympics."

Ron chuckled. He looked at Mike. "When your goal is greater than a medal, it's amazing what you can do."

The kid smiled. "Can I get your picture?"

"Why?" Ron asked.

"I saw you save that guy. You're a hero."

Ron thought back to his own intentions from the day before. He leaned in and whispered to the kid, "He saved me first." As he leaned back, he glanced at Naomi and Mike. The inquisitive looks on their faces indicated they didn't hear what he had whispered.

The teenager had a confounded look. "Um, okay." He backed up, turned around and left.

"What did you say to him?" Naomi asked.

"The truth." Ron smiled.

Her eyebrows furled for a second, but she didn't ask anything more.

Ron picked up his coffee and took another sip. The ship was getting closer to the city coastline. They'd be getting off the boat soon.

"What's next for you guys?" Naomi asked.

"I'd like to get back to the hotel and clean up," Ron said.

"A hot shower," Mike said.

"I bet we're be met by EMTs once we dock," Naomi said. "You two need to get checked out at the hospital."

Mike's stare fell to the floor. "There's probably going to be a police report."

"We'll get through it, Mike," Naomi said.

"Then a shower," Ron said.

"After that, how about dinner tonight," Naomi said. "Like I said earlier, the dinner cruises on the river are great." Mike recoiled, and Naomi laughed at his reaction. "Actually, I was thinking dinner back at Cindy's might be best. What do you say?"

The last of the tension fell away from Mike's face as if in realization he was with friends. "That does sound good." He was no longer shivering.

"I'd have to admit I'm looking forward to getting back home," Ron said. He saw Naomi's face drop. "But I think some time in New York is definitely in my future, too."

Naomi smiled.

"Looking forward to getting back in your own plane?" Mike asked.

Ron nodded.

Mike took another sip of coffee. "That reminds me of something. Let's fly back to Toledo in a few days, if that's all right with you."

"I know a few people in a diner back there I'd like to see again," Ron said.

The smile on Mike's face widened. "Perfect, because I was hoping I could catch a ride with you to a small airport over in Portage County."

"Portage County Airport."

"You know it?"

"Of course. It's just fifteen or twenty minutes north of my home airport."

"If it wouldn't be too much trouble."

Ron saw a gray and white dove feather riding the wind. It tumbled in the air currents which carried it past their table. "No, no trouble at all."

Epilogue

Two Months Later

With heavy eyes, Ron fell back into his bed. Even inside, the night air was cold. Layers of clothing kept him warm beneath layers of covers. In his head, he replayed the phone conversation with Carly from earlier that evening. He looked forward to flying to Toledo the next day to take her and Bradley flying.

His fourth visit to them had occurred a week earlier, and he had promised a tearful Bradley that he'd return soon. Every time Ron was about to leave, the boy teared up, and every time, Ron promised to return.

And every time, Ron returned and kept his promise.

He succumbed to the weight of the day and finally fell asleep.

Ron stood in his backyard. The area was mostly lawn with mature oaks and maples dotted about. The trees were green with young leaves and thick woods shadowed the back perimeter. The sides of the yard disappeared into a dense fog.

His feet felt heavy and solid. He looked down.

"Anne?"

His wife looked up at him. She was squatting next to a box with a dove in it.

"I think she's finally ready to fly again," Anne said as she gingerly picked up the bird.

Ron knelt next to her and slowly shook his head. "Not yet. Let's wait a little longer."

"It's been long enough." Anne stroked the dove and it cooed. "She's ready."

"It's not right to let her go. Not yet."

"Why not? And if not today when?"

"Let's wait until tomorrow."

"Does tomorrow always come?" Her focus remained on the bird as she stroked it.

An unusually warm spring breeze brushed Ron's face. He stood and watched his wife's hair dancing in it.

Anne gazed up at her husband and raised her hands, holding the dove. "Here?"

"What do you want me to do with her?"

"Take her."

"I can't."

"Why not?"

"Because I'm not ready."

"I'm giving her to you. She's yours now."

Ron's breathing increased and his hands felt clammy. He felt a pending panic attack.

"It's okay now. It's time."

With eyes welling with tears, both of them met each other's gaze. Ron reluctantly took the dove and a tremor went down his spine. As he held the dove, his agitation subsided.

"You can do this," Anne encouraged.

Ron gently held the bird. It was like holding air, he could barely feel it in his hands. He gently stroked its back. The bird lowered its head as Ron stroked it with his forefinger.

Ron's eyes filled with emotion. "Are you ready to go?"

The bird tucked itself low in his hands as if to answer.

"It's okay. You can go."

After a few seconds, the bird lifted its head and extended its wings. Then it took off.

Ron watched the dove fly away. It slowly ascended in a large circular pattern. Higher and higher it flew, until it disappeared into the blue sky over the woods.

A small dot in the sky caught Ron's attention. He followed the dot, which became a dove's feather. The wind toyed with it and it drifted lower and lower, until it lay in the grass at his feet beside the empty box.

Anne was gone.

Ron smiled as the tears fell.

The next morning Ron awoke feeling well rested. He wanted to live.